The heat ~~of Lenny's~~
bu~~rning gaze~~

Jane took in a breath. Did he see the loneliness, the isolation of the wall she'd managed to build around herself to keep others out?

Did he see her as a successful life coach, or a pathetic woman who'd come in hopes of using his name and his fame for her own purposes?

"Lenny, I can help clean up your grandmother's house. For her sake. She'd want that, don't you think?"

"You know something, Coach. I'm beyond help. I appreciate your efforts, but you should leave while you've got a chance."

"I don't want to leave," Jane replied. And this time, it had nothing to do with ulterior motives or professional recognition.

Dear Reader,

This book is very special to me because even though I write for Steeple Hill Books, this is my very first Harlequin Superromance novel. I love writing for Steeple Hill Books and hope to continue doing that, but this story was a bit different, so I was thrilled when the editors of the Harlequin Superromance line decided to publish it.

I was born and have lived in the South all my life, and this is a Southern story. My heroine, Jane, lives in Arkansas, a state known for Razorback football, but she hates the game! It makes perfect sense that when she gets the assignment of a lifetime—to use her life-coaching skills to help ex-NFL quarterback Lenny Paxton get over a serious midlife crisis—she'll take the challenge. But Lenny proves to be a hard case and doesn't want to be tamed. These two opposites are definitely attracted to each other. Soon, Lenny has a plan to give Jane a bit of coaching, too.

This quirky Southern story was such fun to write. I'd love to hear what you think. You can contact me through my website—www.lenoraworth.com.

Lenora Worth

Because of Jane
Lenora Worth

HARLEQUIN®

TORONTO • NEW YORK • LONDON
AMSTERDAM • PARIS • SYDNEY • HAMBURG
STOCKHOLM • ATHENS • TOKYO • MILAN • MADRID
PRAGUE • WARSAW • BUDAPEST • AUCKLAND

Recycling programs
for this product may
not exist in your area.

ISBN-13: 978-0-373-71684-5

BECAUSE OF JANE

ABOUT THE AUTHOR

Lenora Worth has written more than forty books for three different publishers. Her career with Steeple Hill Books spans close to fourteen years. Her very first Love Inspired title, *The Wedding Quilt,* won *Affaire de Coeur*'s Best Inspirational for 1997, and *Logan's Child* won *RT Book Reviews*' Best Love Inspired for 1998. With millions of books in print, Lenora continues to write for the Love Inspired and Love Inspired Suspense lines. Lenora also wrote a weekly opinion column for the local paper and worked freelance for years with a local magazine. She has now turned to full-time fiction writing and enjoying adventures with her retired husband, Don. Married for thirty-five years, they have two grown children. Lenora enjoys writing, reading and shopping…especially shoe shopping. This is her first Harlequin Superromance novel.

Books by Lenora Worth

LOVE INSPIRED SUSPENSE

FATAL IMAGE
SECRET AGENT MINISTER
DEADLY TEXAS ROSE
A FACE IN THE SHADOWS
HEART OF THE NIGHT
CODE OF HONOR
RISKY REUNION
ASSIGNMENT: BODYGUARD
THE SOLDIER'S MISSION

STEEPLE HILL

AFTER THE STORM
ECHOES OF DANGER
ONCE UPON A CHRISTMAS
  "'Twas the Week Before Christmas"

†In the Garden
††Sunset Island
*Texas Hearts

LOVE INSPIRED

THE WEDDING QUILT
LOGAN'S CHILD
I'LL BE HOME FOR CHRISTMAS
WEDDING AT WILDWOOD
HIS BROTHER'S WIFE
BEN'S BUNDLE OF JOY
THE RELUCTANT HERO
ONE GOLDEN CHRISTMAS
WHEN LOVE CAME TO TOWN††
SOMETHING BEAUTIFUL††
LACEY'S RETREAT††
EASTER BLESSINGS
  "The Lily Field"
THE CARPENTER'S WIFE*
HEART OF STONE*
A TENDER TOUCH*
BLESSED BOUQUETS
  "The Dream Man"
A CERTAIN HOPE†
A PERFECT LOVE†
A LEAP OF FAITH†
CHRISTMAS HOMECOMING
MOUNTAIN SANCTUARY
LONE STAR SECRET
GIFT OF WONDER
THE PERFECT GIFT
HOMETOWN PRINCESS

To Tara Gavin, Wanda Ottewell
and Patience Smith.
Thanks to each of you for believing in me, pushing
me to be my best and letting me write this story!

And to Steve Miller, of course.

CHAPTER ONE

FROM HIS SPOT atop the hill, Lenny Paxton watched as his friend Henry Powell ran around the old truck to help the passenger. Amusement at Henry's chivalrous antics changed to dread inside Lenny's heart.

It couldn't be. But it was. Henry set suitcases and tote bags down on the dusty road, tipped his hat to the woman standing there. Then with a grin, the man ambled back to the idling vehicle and took off, spinning rocks as he headed on up the mountain road.

"I don't believe this," Lenny said, his words edged with aggravation. He watched as the woman grabbed at her luggage and trudged up the rocky dirt driveway toward the farmhouse, purses and bags falling down her arms.

"Trouble, double trouble," Lenny said, thinking a man could certainly reach his limits on days like this one. He'd just had words with ex-wife number two and now this.

Another woman in his life. An unwelcome, unwanted woman. And most of the women in his life were that way these days. He'd have to nip this in the bud right now.

But the primal male in him shifted gears. She did

look kinda cute carrying all that baggage up that hill. Taking his time, he watched, a trickle of his old wickedness making him smile. He should go help her, but he wasn't nearly as noble as old Henry. "Let her sweat a bit."

Then she swayed, tripped on a rock and popped one of the heels off her pretty pumps. Lenny had to laugh at the words the cute woman uttered. A tad feisty underneath all that gabardine, wasn't she?

When she threw down the bags and held up what was left of the heel of her right shoe, her expression full of exasperation and frustration, in spite of his aversion to the female population right now, Lenny knew he couldn't let this one slide. This might get interesting.

SHE'D BROKEN A HEEL.

Letting out a groan, Jane Harper held that heel and looked up from her now ruined black Italian leather "client-meeting" pumps to the two-storied whitewashed farmhouse sitting with forlorn loneliness up on the hill in front of her. At least she was here now. And from the looks of the place, she'd be here a while. The yard was weed-covered and drought-thirsty. An old International tractor sat lopsided near a giant live oak on a hill, looking like a petrified bug. The steps were cracked, the porch paint was peeling. And the porch was lined with several pieces of vintage wicker furniture and Victorian plant stands, along with exercise equipment and piles of various brands of empty beer cans.

Jane glanced around, hoping the rumors she'd heard about shotguns weren't true. She envisioned this place clean and well repaired. She could see this house renewed and invigorated, shining brightly with fresh white paint and ferns sitting pristinely on those fabulous old stands. She could almost smell freshly baked bread coming from the open kitchen window, hear the sound of someone practicing piano from inside the parlor. She'd plant daisies near that old tractor and make it into a backdrop instead of an eyesore.

Jane's heart hurt for this place. All it lacked was a little nurturing. Her organizational skills were sorely needed. For this house, and for the man who'd been holed up here—allegedly armed and dangerous—since last spring.

"Certainly have my work cut out for me," she mumbled to the broken heel of her pump.

But if anyone could get rid of the clutter surrounding the quaint Victorian house, Jane could. And if anyone could bring former NFL quarterback Lenny Paxton out of his self-imposed isolation after losing the Super Bowl, losing his beloved grandmother and then losing his cool in front of the world, Jane could. She also planned to get the scoop on the story everyone wanted—what in the world was wrong with Lenny Paxton?

Maybe everything that had happened up to now—the long drive from Little Rock, getting a flat tire out on the main road, then meeting the skinny, philosophical Henry in the old red pickup (he'd been kind enough to give her a ride and to warn her that she might get shot) and now her broken heel—had all been signs that she should have stayed in the big city.

Never one to take bad luck as the gospel, Jane dug in her one good heel and worked on calming thoughts. Forgetting her damaged shoe, she stood in the warm sunshine of this fall Arkansas afternoon, sweat pooling underneath her lightweight gray wool dress, steam fogging her black-rimmed glasses. After some steady deep-breathing, she once again looked over the meticulous notes tucked in her leather tote bag.

Subject: Leonard (Lenny) Paxton, former NFL quarterback with two Super Bowl wins to his credit and one big loss still on his mind. Dallas Cowboys, Denver Broncos, multimillion-dollar contracts, messed-up shoulder, messed-up knees, messed-up head, early retirement. Meltdown during a press conference. Now hiding out in the cluttered farmhouse where he'd been raised by his grandparents, refusing to honor the million-dollar endorsement deal he'd signed two weeks after announcing his retirement.

That was the short version.

Jane had the long version in precise typewritten notes in her briefcase and stored in her laptop.

She blew a hot breath up toward the wispy dark blond bangs falling away from what had started out this morning as an efficient chignon. She had her reasons for being here. Reason number one—prestige.

Jane's mother and father had been pushy when it came

to their firstborn. Academic achievements and career aspirations ranked right up there with Arkansas Razorback football fever at the Harper house. Jane had learned from the rigid, structured habits of her overly educated parents. She'd become the perfect overachiever. She'd accomplished a lot of the goals she'd set in her life, but she still needed that one assignment that would push her status to new heights and maybe land her a major book deal.

Too bad the one drawback was that the subject at hand was a jock. Her entire family loved football, and since Lenny had once played for the Razorbacks and had gone on to NFL fame, her University of Arkansas alumni parents would be impressed. But Jane wasn't. Sitting around a football stadium, watching grown men run straight into each other just to capture a strange-looking ball didn't appeal to Jane's delicate sensibilities. And chanting rival fight songs and belching barbecue and beer was not her idea of a great Saturday afternoon. But then, jocks had never flocked to the shy girl who wore glasses and read books instead of swooning like a cheerleader whenever one of them entered the room. If she got the scoop on Lenny Paxton, she'd up her esteem in her parents overly critical eyes.

And that brought her to reason number two. "It's certainly a challenge." Jane loved a challenge. From what she could tell, breaking Lenny Paxton would be both a challenge and a chore. His list of transgressions made for interesting psychological fodder.

Jane took her assignments very seriously. So while her car sat on the interstate with a flat, Henry had promised he'd get the tire changed while she got right to business. And in spite of having a very strong aversion to superjocks and guns, Jane would get Lenny Paxton whipped into shape. Or her name wasn't Jane Harper, Ph.D.

She was efficient, dependable, reliable, thorough, no-nonsense, and she had earned her Ph.D. in Psychology from the University of Arkansas. And even though her academic parents and siblings frowned on Jane's status as a life coach, she had worked with everyone from supermodels to burned-out ministers to stay-at-home moms who needed some self-esteem. And that, Jane Harper reminded herself, was why she got the big bucks. And the exotic assignments. This assignment just might beat the band since she'd received a phone call from the notorious *Sidelined* sports magazine that prided itself on getting the scoop on the most interesting and infamous sport figures in the world.

They wanted her to write an in-depth exposé on Lenny Paxton. Jane had agreed, but only after she'd told the magazine's gleeful editor that she couldn't reveal any client/therapist secrets without the client's permission. While the editor wasn't too happy about that, the man had reluctantly agreed to her doing the article on spec. Now, Jane's main goal was to win over Lenny enough to get him to open up so his inspiring story could help other people.

In spite of the remote, rather quaint location—Mockingbird Springs, Arkansas, population 989—this one had been too tempting to pass up. Famous athlete and ladies' man extraordinaire Lenny Paxton was in trouble. He'd disappointed his team and his fans, and lost his confidence. He'd quickly retired in disgrace only to turn around and sign another contract—this one with a major pharmaceutical company. But now he wanted out of his contract. So his hotshot sports agent, Marcus Ramon, had resorted to drastic measures to get Lenny back on track. He'd called Dr. Jane Harper.

She'd come, after being wooed by Lenny's hyper agent and by *Sidelined* magazine, from Little Rock to this backwoods village to help a man who was having a very public, very intense midlife crisis that he was trying hard to keep private. And because Jane hated jocks and especially hated football, she was going way outside her comfort zone. Only because she knew she could learn from each new experience. And, hopefully, make a name for herself that would please even her discerning parents.

She dropped her briefcase and leather tote, then turned to unzip her suitcase to find a pair of low heeled buttery-soft brown loafers. Then she took off her prized pumps and put them in her tote, broken heel and all.

Better. Not as professional, but a lot more sensible.

Gathering her things along with her pride and some fresh determination, Jane started marching up the dusty drive toward the rambling old house set against the backdrop of the Ozark Mountains. "And reason number three—the money. Always good to get a giant bonus for expediency."

Jane Harper, psychologist and relationship therapist, nonfiction author, authority on the human psyche and all-around consummate life coach and perfectionist might have just taken on the most challenging assignment of her career. She'd probably get network interviews and her name in *People* magazine.

Lenny Paxton was not only a challenge. The man was a walking mess, so macho and such a jock, and so in trouble with everyone from ex-wives and angry girlfriends to just about the entire world of sports media, Jane couldn't wait to take him on.

So she pulled on the handle of her heavy rolling suitcase and took another step toward the inviting comfort of the white rocking chairs sitting amidst the jumble on the wraparound porch.

From inside the house, a dog barked then whimpered as if it were already bored with the quarry walking up the driveway.

Jane hitched a breath. "Great. I'm allergic to dogs." Then she saw the overgrown morning glory bush by the steps. "Now that's pathetic."

From somewhere at the side of the house, a voice barked in what sounded like a very aggravated tone, "Pathetic—now that's a good way to describe this situation."

Jane turned at the smirking words coming from the

deeply male voice. Turned and came face-to-face with
the real-life-legend-in-his-own-time Lenny Paxton. He
was standing underneath an enormous old live oak and
he was holding a very big shotgun.

Jane swallowed back the metallic taste of fear as
she inhaled what she hoped was a steadying breath.
He'd been hidden from view, which meant he'd had
the distinct advantage of studying her before she could
study him. Drat on that, she'd study him now. After all,
that was why she was here. And she wouldn't let that
gun stop her. Mainly because he didn't have it aimed at
her.

Yet.

Dropping her bags, she gave him a long, completely
professional appraisal, from the top of his dark, thick
hair to the tips of his battered, dusty cowboy boots.
Hmm.

Okay, she'd prepared herself for the confounding
variables of this case. One being his lethal charm. She
was *so* immune to that, thanks to the many titillating
articles regarding his love life. Both fascinated and re-
pulsed, she'd pored over them for days on end. Lenny
Paxton was the typical love 'em and leave 'em type—
very predictable and very commitment-shy.

She'd prepared herself for his skeptical nature—or
at least Marcus Ramon had warned her in person to
watch for that—warned her in a loud, shrieking voice,
his hands flapping in the air as he kept stating, "Don't
fall for that dry wit and oozing charm, Jane. It's just a

front for all his cynicism and stubbornness. And for his pain. You have to be professional at all times or *he'll* sideline *you*."

And she thought she'd prepared herself for Lenny's good looks, but mercy, the man was even better-looking in person than in all the pictures she'd managed to dig up from the newspapers, sports magazines and tabloids. In his faded cream-colored T-shirt, tight jeans and scuffed brown cowboy boots, he sizzled white-hot right along with the Indian summer sun hitting the dusty clay at her feet.

And of course, her low blood-sugar dizziness chose that very moment to kick in, making her vision get fuzzy and her legs turn to mush. *Should have had some protein,* Jane thought belatedly.

"Are you all right?" he asked, meeting her disoriented gaze with one of his own, his whole stance so domineering and formidable, she could understand why he'd put fear in the hearts of opponents all across America.

"I was talking to myself," Jane said, rather defensively. *Don't let him smell any fear.* Because she absolutely was not afraid. Anxious to get on with it, maybe. Determined to change his life, definitely. But not afraid. But being nervous was a good thing. It kept her on her toes. She'd faced down worse subjects. But never one who looked so…tempting.

Just to prove she was capable of overcoming temptation, she added, "I like to talk out loud. It helps me to remember things."

He grinned, showing a row of million-dollar white teeth set against the aged tan of his face. "Well, then, don't let me stop you. Go ahead, answer yourself."

Flustered but not defeated, Jane waved a hand in the air then regained her balance. "I'm not that far gone yet."

"Yeah, right."

She watched as he whipped a spiffy cell phone out of the pocket of his jeans and hit a key. "Marcus, you're fired." Then Lenny popped the phone shut, put his gun against the big oak and headed toward her, lifting her tight, efficiently packed suitcase with all the ease of a gorilla.

"You must be way gone, lady, to come all the way here after I specifically told my fool of an agent to stop you." Hoisting the suitcase with one hand, he started toward the house. "For the record—I don't want you here."

"You didn't just fire your agent, did you?"

"I did." He kept walking. "But I fire him once a week for good measure anyway."

She registered his expected hostility and denial. Nothing a little behavior modification and open discussion couldn't fix. "That's terrible. But at least you know who I am and why I'm here."

He gave a short chuckle, his melancholy blue eyes flashing fire. "Oh, yeah, I know who you are, all right. And I can tell you right now, I do not need a life coach and I sure don't need a stranger coming into my home to get it organized. That's the most ridiculous thing I've ever heard." He shook his head at the notion, the skin around his eyes crinkling nicely as he smirked. "Life coach, my—"

"You don't want me here," Jane interrupted, glad to be rid of the heavy suitcase and glad to get the nasty denials out of the way. Hurrying to catch up with his long-legged stroll, she added, "That is perfectly understandable, Mr. Paxton, but I can assure you, we will work through that."

"I'm Lenny, and it is not perfectly understandable," he replied as he stomped on his battered boots toward the house. "I'll put this in my Jeep and we'll get you back on the road to Little Rock, because we don't have anything to work through."

Jane stopped at the bottom step, looking up at where he'd dropped her suitcase amid an old pile of pots and pans on the gray-colored, planked porch floor. "I'm not leaving. Your agent said the judge who presided over your last court hearing and arraignment—for cracking a few heads in a bar in Dallas—specifically said you needed a psychological evaluation. I can give you one and get that judge off your back at the same time. And maybe we can also work through getting this house and your life organized."

He turned to stare down at her with ice-hard disdain. In spite of his freezing look, more sweat beads popped out down her backbone. His voice went deceptively low.

"No, you're not going to analyze me, Ms. Harper. And, yes, you are leaving."

"I can't," Jane replied. "I promised your agent we'd get you in shape for that big endorsement contract. You know, the one with certain stipulations—the first being that you show up sober for the preliminary photo session and press conference and you don't try to back out on the contract that you technically already signed."

LENNY DECIDED he didn't want to play this game after all. "I *didn't* want to sign that contract," he retorted, his reasons for bolting too raw and harsh to explain to this perky stranger. "And I did not agree to this stupid idea that Marcus and some judge concocted about cleaning up my act."

Then he looked out at the autumn-tinged mountains beyond this quiet valley, wondering why he even bothered to explain. She wouldn't care about his newfound insecurities and fears. And he was too much of a man to spill his ugly history to anyone, let alone some skinny shrink who was probably only here to garner a mention in the press, just like everyone else who shadowed him.

"And not that it matters, but I was not drunk that day of the press conference and photo shoot. The night in the bar, yes, but not the day of the press conference."

She put her dainty hands on her dainty hips, reminding Lenny of one of the pretty dolls his grandmother liked to collect. "That's not how the tabloids saw things."

"Yeah, well, the tabloids lie." He shifted, let out a grunt. "I don't need you here, Ms. Harper."

She stared at him with so much clinical intensity, he actually got nervous. "You know something, Lenny, you're an amazing specimen of manhood. So completely male, the testosterone is bouncing off you like laser rays."

"Glad you noticed," he said with a lift of his chin. And a testosterone-filled angry glare.

Score one for Lenny. She touched a hand to her burnished hair, while an equally burnished blush moved down her throat. "All of that aside, you've made a mess of things. You need a life coach."

He said something crude then shook his head. "No, I don't believe I do. I am perfectly fine and I wish my superagent could get that through his thick California skull."

"He's concerned about—"

"He's concerned about the money," Lenny said, coming down the steps to take her briefcase and tote. He handily tossed them up beside her carry-on, oblivious to the crinkle and crash of her files and personal items. "He doesn't want the Lenny Paxton gravy train to end. And I'm pretty sure it's my money he's offering you to come here for this *exclusive* therapy session."

"I wouldn't exactly look at it that way," she said

through a cringe of distaste. "He just hates to see you wasting away."

He lifted his hands then winked at her to hide the bulletlike accuracy of her words. "Do I look like I'm wasting away?"

Looking appalled and attractive, she shook her head. "You look okay. Maybe a little out of shape and you do have dark circles under your eyes. But we can fix that with diet and exercise and meditation, and in just a few weeks."

"A few weeks?" Lenny stomped a foot against the wooden steps, causing caked mud to fall away from his boots. He couldn't handle this kind of talk for that long. "You're not serious?"

"I'm very serious. I came to stay for the duration, since part of my assignment is to go through this place and get it in tip-top shape. Usually it takes about a month, but I'm prepared to stay longer if necessary." Then she leaned forward like a mighty little warrior. "You see, it's not so much about the clutter in the house, but more about the clutter in your head."

He put his hands on his hips then nailed her with what sports reporters called the Paxton Scowl. "Meditation? You're really serious?"

She smiled prettily. "Very."

He scowled nastily. "Really?"

"Really."

"We'll just see about that. I'd hate to resort to shooting a woman."

Her frown wasn't so surefire. "You won't shoot me and you can't send me away. I'm tired and I'm hungry. I drove all day, so I'd have my own car. But I got a flat out on the highway, and Henry came by. I endured Henry's smelly, oil-guzzling old truck and even older Hank Williams eight-tracks. At least let me stay the night, then we can discuss this like two civilized adults."

She sounded so pitiful, Lenny had to challenge her, just because he was in a really bad mood. "Depends on what happens during the night, don't you think?"

Touchdown. She turned as red as Henry's old truck. "I'm here in a professional capacity only, Mr. Paxton."

Lenny figured he could change all that, but refrained from suggesting anything specific for now. "Of course you are, Ms. Harper. Don't worry. You're not really my type anyway."

His cell phone rang. "Henry?" Lenny gave Jane a cool look. "Yes, Henry, she really is a life coach. No, I didn't shoot her, and no, I'm not keeping her." He hung up. "Henry sends his regards and said to tell you he's already changed the flat tire. He'll bring the car around sooner or later."

"That was nice of him," Jane replied. "I didn't have a spare."

"Yeah, Henry's real nice. And you should always carry a spare."

He went back up the steps and stared at her tote and briefcase. Because some of her pens and paper clips had fallen out, he bent to pick them up and shove them back inside her bag, his hand clutching her tube of "Cinnamon Sweet" lipstick a little too long. When he stood, he tried to hide the pain shooting throughout his body. No need to let her see how he'd been battered and bruised in the name of football. And no need for her to see into his battered and bruised soul, either.

But she noticed anyway. Her tone hinted of understanding and sympathy. "I can't leave. You look as if you need someone to talk to and I'm tired and I need a solid meal. Please?"

Lenny wanted to be mean and tell her to take a hike, but he couldn't do that to a stranded woman, even if he really didn't want to deal with another woman. "Fine, then. Make yourself at home, but just for tonight."

He pointed toward the screen door. "There's a big room upstairs on the right." He paused, looked out toward the mountains again, thinking he'd regret putting her in that particular room, but at least it was clean. "I guess you can stay in there, but you'd better not rearrange anything, understand? The kitchen is straight down the hallway to the left." Leaning close, he added, "And don't expect room service."

LENNY MARCHED past Jane, the smell of sweat and spice surrounding him in a heated mist that hit her nostrils with all the force of something both forbidden and enticing. Since when had her sensory awareness escalated to the point of bringing on an adrenaline rush? Just nerves and being tired, she told herself as she watched his retreating back.

"You have a dog in there, right?"

He turned, a wolfish grin causing his words to come out in a snarl. "Yeah. I hope you like animals, because the dog stays—but you won't be here long enough to get to know my dog, or me."

Memo to self, Jane thought, watching the frown increase on his face. *This man is hostile and unyielding.* Marcus hadn't told her Lenny didn't want her here. Marcus hadn't told her a lot of things. Such as, this man was obviously hurting in more than just a physical way.

"Thank you for letting me stay," Jane called after him, a nervous twitch forming over her left eyebrow. "You *won't* regret this."

"I already do," he shot back, his tone dismissive and condescending. "Just leave your bags there. I'll bring them up later."

Then he picked up his gun and disappeared around the side of the house.

Jane turned toward the cool darkness of the hallway beyond the screen door, dragging her bags since she was certainly capable, for goodness' sake. There she was met by the biggest, ugliest dog she'd ever seen. A dog that immediately started drooling on her loafers.

CHAPTER TWO

"UH, OH." Jane did not like animals. Animals were smelly and slobbery and usually an all-around pain in the neck (just like football players, come to think of it). Her eyes already burning, she said, "Get off me, you big lug."

Taking her verbal plea as an invitation, the dog pawed his way up her dress, whimpering for attention. Jane grabbed his dirty paws, desperate to get him away from her personal space. "I said, get off me." She backed against the screen door, causing it to squeak and creak. Grabbing onto the doorjamb, she tried to save the last of her dignity before Lenny found her standing here, cowering.

But it was too late. The groaning door gave way while the dog kept advancing toward her. Jane backed up, her hand slipping from the doorjamb while the screen door banged open.

She fell back against Lenny Paxton's hard chest, felt the solid wall of his body and immediately felt a charged current of energy radiating from him. Before she could pull away, the dog came running and crashed into her—front side. While Lenny held her—back side.

"Boy!"

At Lenny's harsh command, the dog dropped, whimpered a retort then gave Jane a big-eyed look as if to say, "Aren't I lovable enough for you?"

Jane looked around at the man fogging up her usually sensible brain right along with her really sensible glasses. Lenny lifted her away, his movements shaking the old floorboards of the porch, his famous frown locked inches from her nose.

Looking just about as flustered as she felt, he said, "I told you I have a dog."

"Is that what this is?" she managed to ask through a shaky laugh, her eyes on the huge monstrosity sitting at her feet. "More like an ox."

Judging from the smirk on his face, Lenny was enjoying her discomfort. But Jane also saw something else in his diamond-edged eyes. Fear and apprehension. He'd done this on purpose. Let her walk right into this big animal. His scare tactics weren't going to drive her away, just because he was afraid to have her here. She'd take an allergy pill and get along with this big brute. And the dog, too.

To prove she was in this for the long haul, Jane wiped her sweaty hands on her dress then leaned over and tentatively patted the dog on its splotchy gold-and-white head. "Nice doggy. What a nice fellow."

Lenny gave her a once-over, surprise settling on his face like a flag falling after a football play. "Boy—his name is Boy. And he's harmless but overly friendly. It's part of his charm." He smiled as if to say it was also part of *his* charm. Then he lifted her bags to settle them in a spot by the stairs.

At least her bags were advancing, even if she wasn't.

Jane followed, stepping around groaning bookcases and ancient sideboards stacked with dishes and dolls, hoping to open a dialogue. "Boy? Your dog's name is Boy?"

Lenny shrugged, stalked to the refrigerator in the long, multi-windowed kitchen. This room had a lot of country charm, all frilly and old-fashioned and overdone with roosters of various sizes. And more dishes, along with cabinets filled with pots and pans, and more dolls on some of the counters. The only saving grace—the big windows were thrown open to allow the crisp fall breeze to play through the lacy white curtains.

Lenny Paxton looked as out of place in here as a gladiator in a queen's sitting room. Which only added to his mystique. Why had he come to this particular place in this particular time of his life? And how could someone so intimidating and burly live with all this dainty stuff?

Jane jotted copious notes in her writing pad. When Lenny turned around, she hid the pad then pushed at her glasses. "Boy?" she repeated, trying to work up some meaningful discussion. Since he seemed to love the dog, she decided to start with that. Except that every time she said "Boy" the dog looked at her with hopeful expectation. The man did not.

"Yes, his name is Boy." He patted the dog's head. "It was the only thing he'd answer to when my granddaddy found him up on the highway. It kinda stuck." He looked out over the big backyard. "Granddaddy died about a year after he found Boy."

Jane registered that information and the reverent way he'd told her, since she hadn't been able to find out much about his early years. Famous she could research; private, what-makes-you-tick stuff was harder to investigate. "I'm sorry. Were you close to your grandfather?"

He turned with another attempt at a smirk, his hostility bouncing off the walls like the beats of a big brass drum. "You are not going to get any fodder out of me, so don't even try. I don't have any issues. I'm perfectly content. Or at least I was until you got here."

"Sorry. I was trying to be polite."

Lenny gave her a long, curious stare, then nodded toward the dog still hassling at her feet. "At least Boy seems to trust you. But then, he's dumber than dirt."

"What exactly *is* he?" Jane asked as she brushed off her dress. She could feel the hives working their aggravating way up her neck. Thankfully, she had a good supply of hand sanitizer and allergy pills in her bag.

"Part hound, part collie, I think."

"Are you sure there isn't some wolf and wild boar mixed in there somewhere?"

That actually made the man smile. He had a nice, devastating smile.

Clearing her throat, Jane watched as he took a vintage Fiestaware pitcher out of the refrigerator then poured some water into a plastic Razorback cup. Pushing at the various dishes, he found a dainty crystal glass and filled it with water then shoved it at her. "Drink this."

Jane took the water, watching as he picked up the plastic cup then lifted it in a salute. When he downed the whole thing, desire flooded through her system with a thousand-watt brilliance. Desire for the water, not the man, she assured herself. And just to prove that point, she also downed part of her glassful.

He turned, stared at her as if she were in the way then shrugged again. "I'm so sorry. Where are my manners? We need to sit down and talk about how to get you back to wherever it is that shrinks go to roost."

He was playing hard to get, siccing his dog on her, making insults. Typical hostile male behavior. Meaning this would not be a good time to tell him she was also on assignment with *Sidelined* magazine. "Just pass the water jug again, would you? I'm hot and tired, and the least you can do is allow me the courtesy of your time. I might be able to help you if you give me a chance."

He stood back, his intimidating crystal eyes shot full of misgivings. "Is this one of those shrink games? A trick to make me change my mind?"

"No, absolutely not," she said, advancing a step. Boy followed her, stopping whenever she stopped. She didn't like playing the helpless female, but Jane had to try a different tactic with this one. "I was counting on this assignment. I like the money, of course, and I need some time away from my other patients." Almost to herself, she added, "They're really getting on my nerves."

He arched his thick eyebrows, his nostrils flaring as if he'd just sniffed something in the air. "I thought it was your job to *keep* people from going crazy."

"It is. I mean, I do. Actually, I just help people to gain self-esteem and get rid of some excess baggage in both their personal and emotional lives. I've written books, based on some of my experiences, with my clients' permission, of course." She glanced around at the ceramic roosters filling the kitchen, her fingers itching to straighten things about as bad as the hives on her neck were itching to be scratched.

"Don't count on doing that with me," he retorted, his tone quiet and deadly, even with lace curtains lifting behind him in the afternoon breeze.

"Uh…well…it's not just that," she said, wondering if she'd ever gain his trust. "Sometimes, it's good to get out of the office now and then." Rummaging through her purse, she found her allergy pills, took one with the water then sat the glass on the one clear spot amid the sports magazines and obvious unopened bills on the table.

Lenny cranked up a portable CD player sitting on the counter. Steve Miller's "Abracadabra" filled the air. "Running from something, doc?"

Jane realized her mistake. Lenny Paxton thought she was too wacky to advise anyone. And maybe he was right. She was a klutz at times. And she did have her own issues. Especially regarding jocks. She was so not a jock-type woman.

Reminding herself to stay professional, she pushed at her chignon. "Could I sit down, please?"

He found a clear chair—all chrome and red aged vinyl—then with a flourish, lifted his hands toward her and said in a sarcastic tone, "By all means, sit, take a load off."

Jane urged her tired bones toward the cushioned chair. Didn't this house have air-conditioning? In spite of the cool breeze coming from the window, she felt flushed.

"Thank you," she said, taking in the old, linoleum-topped breakfast table. Then she sank against the table, causing its chrome legs to scrape across the wooden floor. "I didn't want to be a part of all the Razorback hoopla back in Little Rock. My family tends to take game day very seriously."

He grinned the way a warrior with a spear would grin as he went in for the kill. "You don't like football?"

Jane stood up straight, trying to focus, trying to reach the volume dial on the CD player. "Not at all."

Lenny pushed her hand away. "But you came here anyway, to fix me? Or is that it? You hate football, so it's your goal to fix all football players?"

She cleared her tight throat. "It's a paying assignment,

regardless of the unpleasant subject matter." Then Boy decided to make another play for her. Gasping, Jane backed up against the chair. And got dizzy again.

Lenny caught her by her elbows, then frowned an inch away from her face. "What ails you, anyway?"

"I...missed lunch."

"Sit down," he said, shoving her onto the chair. "You obviously aren't used to this late-summer heat." His mock-concerned look didn't give her hope that the man did have a heart.

"I grew up in Arkansas," she pointed out, a triumphant tone in her voice to undermine her wobbly legs. "I know all about heat and humidity. It's rather nice out today and the leaves are just starting to turn." She smiled, squirmed, looked away. "All in all, rather enjoyable. In fact, I'd forgotten how lovely the fall leaves are."

"Too bad you won't get to stick around. Fall in the Ozarks is really pretty. That is, when you're out in the peace and quiet of the country."

"All the more reason to be here, instead of cooped up in my office back in the city."

He made a sad face. "If only you could stay."

"Let's forget all about that for now. Did *you* grow up in Arkansas?"

He didn't answer. Instead he slapped her question back at her. "Did you grow up in Little Rock, or just find a place to roost there and hang out your shingle?"

"Yes, I grew up in Little Rock," Jane replied, trying

to be honest in hopes that he'd do the same. "My dad was in the air force so we traveled a lot, but when he retired we settled back in Arkansas. My parents are both college professors now. We moved to Fayetteville when I was in high school. They taught at the University of Arkansas there for years."

And she'd been an awkward, geeky teenager who'd babysat instead of going to homecoming and prom. "So my family—I have a sister and a brother, both younger than me—are all Trojan and Razorback fans. My parents moved back to Little Rock a few years ago, and during football season, everyone congregates for football parties. Everyone but me, unless I'm forced to do so."

"Wow, you really do hate football. Isn't it sacrilege to miss a Razorback game?"

Jane felt the need to defend her position. "I work a lot. I keep a private practice, and my self-help books and magazine articles are doing quite well. I lecture at major companies, help train employees, get people motivated to live their best lives. I can do the same for you."

He ignored that suggestion. "Why didn't you move— say to New York or Los Angeles? You know, some place where all the really crazy people live?"

"I love Arkansas," she said, not even daring to voice her real reasons for staying close to home.

The music ended and he didn't move a muscle, but the tension in the room seemed to tighten with each breath Jane took. Lenny Paxton sure wasn't the chatty type, and so far she'd shared more with him than she had intended. Which only made Jane want to question *him*. But she held her ground, smiling up at him with what she hoped was a serene demeanor.

He came toward the table then leaned down to plant both his big hands across the faded linoleum, his buff body hovering inches from her. Then he smiled, another real honest-to-goodness smile, but his tone was low and drawling, his eyes bright with a dare. "A southern girl. I like southern girls. And I especially like home-grown Arkansas girls."

Jane pulled back. He was too close, way too close. She did not like people getting in her face. Or her space. "Could I have some more water, please?"

He pushed off the table, poured the water then turned to watch her. "See, I told you…even though the wind is cool, that sun is still hot. I think it addled your brain. You look flushed."

"I'm fine, really." Sweat poured all the way down to her toes, but she didn't dare tell him that, especially with him looking at her as if he'd just met his next conquest and he'd already won. "My trip across the state was a bit rough."

"All the more reason for you to *not* be here," he replied as he handed her another glass of water. "Want a piece of peach pie?"

Jane's stomach lurched at the mention of food, and at the way he'd changed from disagreeable to debonair. "No, I…I have a delicate stomach. I think something at the truck stop—"

"You should never eat truck stop food."

"I didn't. I skipped breakfast and lunch, but I grabbed a cup of something that resembled coffee and I had half a Luna bar in my car."

"Some coach you are," he retorted, reaching for a loaf of what looked like fresh-baked bread. "I'm gonna butter this and toast it for you and you're gonna eat, okay?"

"Okay."

She wasn't used to being ordered around, but she was hungry. She should have eaten. Low blood-sugar and all that. But she was surprised by his abrupt need to feed her. Was it part of his obvious compulsions, in the same way his hoarding things around him seemed to be? Deciding to test that theory, she said, "Could you put some cheese on it? I need some protein and calcium."

He gave her a perturbed look and then busied himself with cutting the bread, buttering it, laying the cheese down in precise order and finding a broiler pan, his actions methodical and organized. "You're too skinny."

"Thank you so much."

"I'm just stating the obvious."

At least they were making polite (well, polite on her part, anyway) conversation. She would have to build his trust one affirmation at a time. The man was notorious for his skepticism. And he had an ego the size of Texas. He had ticked off coaches and reporters across the country with his glib attitude and his blunt retorts, and he'd infuriated women on a global level with his definite lack of commitment. A tough case.

So why the need for perfection with the grilled cheese sandwich?

"You don't have to put too much butter on the bread."

He glared at her, looked back at the sandwich and then looked at the trash can.

"Don't throw it away," she said, knowing he wanted to do that very thing. "I'm too hungry to wait for another one."

One compulsion won out over the other. He finished cooking the sandwich, but he kept lifting it with the spatula to stare at it.

Jane was sure she could handle anything this man tried to dish out. But she couldn't help but admire his backside as he buttered that bread and crisped that sandwich.

About an hour later, after one perfect grilled cheese sandwich and a glass of sweet lemonade, Jane felt refreshed, but sleepy. That surprised her. She didn't require much sleep. Maybe it was just the way the breeze moved through those lacy curtains, or the way Boy sighed in his doggy slumber at her feet. Or maybe she needed to rest and try to get her brain back on task, instead of wondering why Lenny had hidden himself away behind clutter here on this remote farm for eight months, when the world was waiting for his next move.

Pace yourself, she thought. *You just got here. Plenty of time to get inside his head.* If she could get past all that indifference and male-speak.

The good news—Lenny stayed with her while she ate. The bad news—he was reading the paper and listening to more Steve Miller—"Jet Airliner" this time—instead of talking to her. Although she couldn't be sure if the issue he was reading was current since the small table was full of all types of publications.

She glanced through the arched kitchen opening toward the hall to the right into a formal dining room/living room combination, wondering why this house was part dainty organization and part mixed-up male. "Tell me about your grandmother, Lenny."

LENNY LIFTED HIS GAZE toward her, then checked his watch. Exactly fifteen minutes. That's how long she'd stayed quiet. He'd almost expected her to fall asleep right there at the table. No such luck. "Who wants to know?"

Shaking a finger at him, she said, "Well, I do. She had a lot of things from what I can see. Was she a collector?"

Deciding he'd best make hay while the sun was shining and answer some of her annoying questions, he said, "Yes, she collected antiques and junk and…dolls."

That was an understatement. This old house looked like a flea market. Lenny knew things looked bad. Okay, worse than bad. But he just didn't have the energy to deal with that right now. And he didn't have the energy to get to the bottom of his new anxieties either. So he let all the collected things sit, neat and tidy, while he kept piling his messy things all around them. The clutter brought him a small measure of comfort. The questions from the perky woman across the table did not.

"What was her name?"

"Bertie." He went back to pretending to read the paper. And put up a solid wall around his pent-up emotions.

"And how long do you plan to keep all of her things around?"

"Forever."

Jane leaned forward, his noncommunicative mood seeming to bounce off her like sun rays. "Why did you walk away after losing the Super Bowl, Lenny?"

He looked up at her and saw the earnestness in her eyes, but Lenny put on his game face. At first, he didn't answer. Then he said, "I was tired." That admission seemed to make him feel a whole lot better about things. Maybe he did need therapy, after all. But who would believe him? The whole world had given up on Lenny Paxton.

"You look tired now. You have dark circles under your eyes. Do you sleep at all?"

Lenny's brand of tired creaked all the way to his bones. He couldn't remember the last time he'd had a good night's sleep. "I get by," he said. "But I suppose you can help me find some new energy?" Exploring the possibilities of that proposition did intrigue him. Analyze a little bit; flirt a little bit. See which one of them caved first. That tactic had always garnered him a pretty woman on his arm. But then, maybe he didn't have the energy to even flirt.

"That's part of the therapy, yes."

He watched as she started stacking magazines, clearing away the section of the table she had somehow managed to take over. "Even if you think you're too old for football, even if you don't get this current contract dispute settled, you *could* be a commentator or a spokesperson. Your agent says you've got offers all over the place, endorsement deals, movie offers—"

His halfway good mood turned to ice as a kind of panic knocked the wind out of him. "My agent—the one I just fired—talks too much and presumes too much. Those deals aren't worth the paper they're written on. Most of them are comical or beneath my dignity. I'm not ready for stupid reality shows about has-beens." He flipped open his phone, then shook his head. "Eight messages from Marcus already. Got him backed against a wall." Then he closed the phone but kept his bravado. "I'll let him stew a little bit more." Getting up, he cleared away their dishes. "Oh, and did I tell you—you're fired, too."

Jane got up, whirling and almost running into him as he turned from putting the dishes in the sink. He brought his hands up to block her at the same time she brought her arms out to keep from ramming against him. Their fingers touched.

Lenny felt as if he'd taken a direct hit from some force of nature. Worse than a linebacker coming at him.

Her sleepiness seemed to disappear as her eyes opened in a rush of pure awareness. *His* very cells zinged with a renewed energy. And he didn't feel so tired anymore.

Lenny backed away, while Jane looked startled, her hazel eyes changing like the leaves outside. "Sorry," he said in a deep-throated grunt, the scent of her floral perfume hitting him.

"I...it was my fault." Her jittery laugh caught in her throat. "My father always said I was clumsy. Always rushing, running into things, banging my knees, scraping my hands, falling, always falling."

"I don't see that." His gaze took a stroll down the tiny length of her. "You seem very sure of yourself." He held her hands, looking down at her taupe-colored nail polish. "And your hands don't seem to be all scraped and battered, not like mine, anyway."

She turned his hands in hers, her touch as gentle as the brush of a soft wind, her gaze following the deep calluses on his fingers, the surgery scars on his wrist.

"You do have a lot of scars. Football is not a kind sport."

If only you knew.

"Battle scars," he retorted, trying to hide behind the ice again. But with her tiny hands holding his, Lenny felt something solid and rigid slipping into a slow melt inside him. Acknowledged it and held it back. He couldn't open that floodgate. Not yet. With a gentle tug, he removed his hands from hers. "We all have battle scars, don't we, darlin'?"

JANE TOOK IN A BREATH, the lingering heat of Lenny's calloused touch burning through her. Then, because he was staring at her, she wondered what he really saw when he looked at her. Did he see the unmarried, nearly middle-aged woman who'd given her life to her education and her career? Did he see the loneliness, the isolation of the wall she'd managed to build around herself to keep others out, but more importantly to hold herself in?

Did he see her as the successful life coach, or the pathetic woman who'd come traipsing up his driveway on a broken shoe heel in hopes of using his name and his fame for her own purposes? The woman who worked to keep her own sorry personal life at bay, who stayed close to family simply because she needed the noise they could provide? Appalled, Jane wondered why was she analyzing herself instead of the subject at hand.

"Hey, are you all right?" Lenny asked, his icy eyes turning warm.

"I'm fine. The food helped." Then she put her hands down by her side. "Lenny, please let me help get this place in order. I can help clean up your grandmother's house. For her sake. She'd want that, don't you think?"

His expression turned taut and pinched. "Maybe *I* don't want to get this place in order."

"But you need to get *your* life in order. I can help you with that. And I think you'll feel better afterward."

He shook his head. "You know something, Coach. I'm

beyond help. I appreciate your efforts, but you should leave while you've got a chance."

"I don't want to leave," Jane replied. And this time, it had nothing to do with ulterior motives or professional recognition. And why had that plan changed? she wondered.

Because this bitter, melancholy man has you all twisted and confused, she thought, anger clouding her better judgment. *And you don't get twisted and confused.*

She was about to tell him to stop playing his flirty little head games with her when an alarm went off on his watch. Boy jumped up from his spot at the back door, barking at the buzzing noise.

And then Jane noticed something really amazing about big, bad Lenny Paxton. He looked up the hallway, his consistent frown changing with all the beauty of a cloud passing through the sun's rays, his eyes going from cold and distant to bright and full of excitement.

"What time is it?" he asked as he hit his watch. "This thing is slow sometimes."

Jane looked around at all the various clocks in the kitchen. Not one of them was working. "It's four-thirty."

Lenny made a whistling sound. "This infernal expensive watch has never worked. I have to go feed the hogs before I go to football practice."

Noting his stress coming and going, she said, "Hogs? You have hogs?"

"It's a farm," he said, his words long and drawn out so she could catch on.

"You're going to feed the hogs, before... *What...?* Did you say football practice?"

"Peewee football," he said, grabbing her by the hand. "We have practice and I can't be late. C'mon, you can help."

"With the hogs?"

Lenny nodded, clearly proud of himself for thinking up this idea. "Yeah, and then, Miss Life Coach, you're going to sit tight while I go to practice. This week we have opening night for the Warthogs and I'm their head coach. If you're still around later in the week and if you behave, I might let you go to the game."

If you're still around... He was thinking of letting her stay! A good sign. But about the immediate plans...

Jane backed away. "I don't do hogs and I don't do football."

Lenny turned to lean down, his nose level with hers, his eyes sparkling like fireflies at midnight. "Then what are you doing in Razorback country, lady?"

CHAPTER THREE

JANE WENT UPSTAIRS and entered the first room on the left, her mind reeling. After she'd stood there dumbfounded, her throat too dry to speak, he'd told her to change her clothes. Then he'd dumped her suitcases up here. "Hurry up. We're burning daylight."

After meeting him on the rather narrow stairs—or at least the stairs seemed narrow with him blocking her and with all the clutter of old newspapers and magazines on almost every step—she'd silently watched him stomping away with a parting shot over his shoulder. "Wear something sensible—like jeans and a work shirt."

"I don't have a work shirt. I mean, I have blouses and jeans, and workout clothes, of course, but what exactly kind of shirt do you mean?"

His smirk had deepened as he turned, one hand on the newel post, those crystal blue eyes sweeping over her. "I mean something to keep the bugs off. I'll find you one of mine. Oh, and we might run across some other varmints. You know, snakes, mice. All kinds of critters hang out around the hog pen."

The man was testing her endurance again. She'd thought they might have reached the first breakthrough there in the kitchen, but this was going to take a while. But she was organized and thorough and after having seen where Lenny's priorities were, she knew this mission was important. Lenny needed to learn to let go. And she was the perfect woman to teach him exactly how to do that. As long as she could keep her own scattered reactions to the man at bay.

"I'll be down shortly," Jane had countered, the dare in her words unmistakable. "I can't wait to see the little piggies."

Now, unable to stop the rapid progression of her thoughts, she got out her laptop to make notes on her first impression of Lenny Paxton. Good thing she always carried a tiny tape recorder and notebooks. In five minutes, she'd done a passable first draft of her analysis and saved it on both the hard drive and a flash drive. She'd pretty things up for the magazine article.

Pushing her guilt about that aside, she rushed around stripping off her business clothes with one hand while she talked into the tiny machine which she held in her other hand.

"Subject seems unwilling to try therapy. Concerned that he might be hostile toward working through his problems. (Big surprise, that!) Note: He did make me some food and he can be very pleasant when he sets his mind to it. But it's all an act, I think. He needs to clean up his clutter, both emotionally and in his physical residence. Messy and overstuffed in both areas! Subject seems extremely attached to his grandmother's possessions. Refusal to maintain contact with friends and coworkers indicates a deep-seated need to connect with something from his past—something he has lost." She stopped, took a long breath. "Saw a bit of hope when he turned soft and told me I should leave. It wasn't a threat. It was more of a plea. I think I've made a hint of progress. And for that reason, I think I need to stay."

A paradox, Jane thought as she shut off the tape machine then put it on the old walnut chest of drawers. Lenny looked so out of place in this bulging antique-filled house. And yet, he seemed right at home here, too.

"I think he has a heart," Jane said as she pulled on an old pink T-shirt she'd brought to sleep in. "I intend to find that heart and get it back into shape. And I also intend to find out why Lenny refuses to get back into action. Does he truly want to retire from all public life, or is he just scared of failing? Does this cluttered house bring him comfort, or keep him from going through his real feelings? He's stuck in the past so he can't commit to the future."

No way was she leaving now. This challenge was too important, for her career and also…for Lenny.

Suddenly excited about the prospect of helping Lenny to deal with his problems, Jane delved into her findings with renewed energy. She quickly plugged in her 3G Internet card and pulled up information on hog farms, scribbling notes and making faces about what the poor animals had to endure. Soon, she had information on peewee football, too. She might be a fish out of water, but she could swim upstream if need be.

A loud knock followed by Lenny's bellowing voice brought her head up. "How long does it take to put on a pair of pants, Coach?"

"Oh, I'm almost ready," Jane said, grabbing the jeans she'd tossed on the bed. He'd called her Coach—a term of acceptance if she'd ever heard one. That was a good sign, a very good sign.

ABOUT AN HOUR LATER, Jane wondered if she'd died and gone down below. It was that hot and miserable and stinky in the pigpen. And these animals—brutes, all of them! They snorted and pushed and gobbled and drooled in such disgusting, sickening ways. And the stench! Wishing she had on a protective face mask, Jane tried not to inhale too deeply as she distributed grain, old fruit and wilted vegetables to a passel of grunting, rooting animals.

This was not exactly the industrial-sized operation of a real pig farm; it was more like a few sows and one very-pleased-with-himself, ton-sized boar hog who'd obviously sired the twenty or so squeaking, squealing piglets of various sizes and shapes. No, this was more like an old-fashioned pigsty.

And it smelled worse than anything Jane had ever sniffed in her life.

Reminding herself that she had to get through this first test in order to show Lenny she had staying power,

Jane tossed more pig feed into a dirty metal trough and waited for the onslaught of muddy sows and squealing older piglets. Gingerly stepping out of the way, she turned to survey the round pigpen. This was the last of the feed and every trough had been filled. Her work here was done.

Turning with a satisfied smile on her face, she saw Lenny sitting on the wood-and-wire fence, grinning at her, the smirk of his trickery evident on his face.

"How's it going out there, Coach?"

Jane held her pristine smile in place, in spite of the thumping beat of elevated blood pressure in her temples. "Just dandy." She sneezed. "These piglets are so adorable." Then she added a few choice suggestions. "Tell me, though, have you ever considered using sow stalls or gestation crates to lower your birth production costs? And what about iron? Are these piglets getting daily doses? You know, you could probably produce a better pig if you take my advice."

The proud smirk left Lenny's face as he hopped off the fence and came stomping through the mud toward her. "This isn't some mass market pig farm, Ms. Harper. This is just me—trying to do what my granddaddy always did—raise a few animals for meat."

Jane gasped. "For meat? You mean you're going to send all of these cute little pink pigs to the slaughterhouse."

His laugh was as coarse as a hog's snort. "Of course.

That's what the fancy farms do. Or did you think I was raising them for pets?"

Jane glanced around, eyeing one particular little runt who couldn't seem to get anywhere with either the grain or his mama sow's offers of dinner. "But, Lenny, look at him. He's so precious. You can't mean to send him into such a horrible death."

"Now don't go all PETA on me," Lenny said, reaching out to take the empty grain bucket from her. "This is just a way of life on the farm. Always has been."

"But Precious there shouldn't have to give his life just so you can have bacon for breakfast."

He glared at her then frowned at the struggling little piggy. "That pig's getting all he needs from his mother. He's growing up just fine. I let him out of the stall last week. He'll be all right until he's full grown. So stop worrying over him like an old mother hen. Besides, that sow isn't exactly fawning all over the little runt."

"You obviously know nothing about a mother's love for her child," Jane said, trying to find his sensitive side.

That tack didn't work.

His glare changed into a look Jane would never forget. He stepped toward her, then stepped back, his face red with anger, his eyes igniting in a blue-colored flame. "You have no idea what I know about that," he said as he reached to yank the bucket from her.

Jane held it back, realizing she'd stumbled onto something that Lenny had buried deep inside himself. "I'd like to know all about you."

"I'm warning you to stop," Lenny said. "Don't ask me another question. I don't want you picking my brain."

She had one more question that needed to be asked. "About clutter or your mother?"

That did it. He grabbed for the bucket while Jane stepped backward to keep it from him. Just as he caught at the old, dirty bucket, his foot slipped in the slimy mud. He moved in slow motion toward Jane, his hand reaching for her arm. Then she started slipping with him, right into the middle of all the piglets.

Jane tried to stop the fall, but it was too late. And Lenny, realizing what was about to happen, tried to keep them both balanced. But his efforts were in vain. All he could do was hold on as they both slid with a sickening thud right into the dirty wallow of pig heaven.

"Oh, no," Jane screamed as the bucket went in one direction and her legs went in the other. "Lenny!"

He held her close enough to manage to take the brunt of the fall, but before it was over they were tangled together in wet, coffee-colored mud. With squealing, pushing hogs and pigs all around them.

Jane looked up to find Lenny's eyes on her, his expression bordering on confused and contrite. "Are you all right?" he asked, huffing as he tried to sit up.

But he kept slipping back down and taking her with him. Jane screamed then tried to stand. She felt as if she were caught in quicksand. "Uh, oh. I can't—"

Then they heard a deep-bellied grunt, followed by the sound of agitated boar flesh heading in their direction.

"Lenny?" Jane managed to point with one mud-caked finger toward the boar. "Is he mad?"

Lenny glanced over his shoulder then said something underneath his breath. "You bet he's mad. And so am I."

But, mad or not, he found the strength to pull both of them out of the mire. "Get behind me," he shouted as he tried to block her from the rooting boar.

Jane did as he said, while Lenny grabbed the bucket and threw it to ward off the attack.

"Now what?"

"Now, we run," Lenny shouted as he pushed her toward the fence. "Go! Run now!"

She did, her loafers heavy with clinging mud, her breath leaving her body in a burst. She cleared the fence just as the male hog charged at Lenny. Lenny sprinted to the right, groaning as his leg apparently twisted. Jane went out the unlocked gate, turning to hold it for Lenny to pass through while Boy barked and ran in circles behind her. Lenny used some more of his impressive football moves to zigzag away from the angry boar, then ran through the open gate, grabbing it to push it shut just before the massive animal slammed at it. Jane saw the white of the mad hog's eyes and smelled the stench of his breath, but now there was a fence between them at least.

"You did it. We're safe."

Winded and dirty, Lenny and Jane fell on the grass outside the dirt pen, looked at each other, then burst into laughter.

Then Lenny turned toward her, triumph replacing his earlier anger. "So, had enough? Are you leaving now?"

"No way," she said, determination replacing her fear of hogs. Her family lived for taking dares. And Jane was up to this one. "I'm just getting started."

He gave her a long, muddy look that turned from triumphant to calculating. "I tell you what, Coach. How 'bout you and me make a deal?"

Jane didn't like the challenging dare in *his* eyes. The way he looked at her made her insides quiver like that mud they'd just fallen into. Because she was wet and it was getting cool as dusk descended on them, and because she was wearing one of his old shirts, she shivered. "What kind of deal?"

"You can stay for a little while—just a little while— and…uh…coach me back into shape."

"I can?"

"If you let me do a little coaching with you."

"*I* don't need a coach," she said, turning to get up.

His mud-splattered hand on her arm stopped her. "Oh, yes, ma'am, you most certainly do. You look as uptight as a porcupine."

That unflattering image didn't set well with Jane. "I am not uptight. I'm a professional."

"Yeah, too professional if you ask me." He pulled her up to her feet, his hands on her arms, his eyes a smoky blue now. "I think we could both learn from this situation."

"You do?"

He nodded, then shot her one of his famous Lenny Paxton lady-killer looks. "Oh, yeah. You know, you scratch my back, I'll scratch yours? Could be fun."

"I don't like it," she said. But the memories of his touch made her mind play little tricks on her. "I didn't come here to fraternize, Lenny."

He let her go, slapping his hands together to get rid of mud. "Suit yourself. In that case, you will be leaving the premises first thing tomorrow morning." He whistled for Boy. The big dog came running from where he'd just taken a muddy dip in the pond.

"But—"

Lenny stomped away. "No buts. I might need help getting organized and maybe I need help with this mess I've made of my life, too. But it's my way or the highway. Might as well mix a little pleasure with our business."

The man was giving her an ultimatum?

Anger flared hot and fast inside her system. "Oh, that is so not fair." She didn't need *him* coaching her. That wasn't how this was supposed to work.

He whirled with athletic ease in spite of the mud weighing down his clothes. "No, what is *not fair* is that you had to come here and harass me just because my agent thinks I'm having a midlife crisis."

"Aren't you?" Jane hurried to him, her mind clicking with precision. He thought he'd scare her away with all that charisma and charm and…nearness. But his challenge just made Jane more determined than ever. "All right. I'll take you up on that deal. Then we'll see who needs coaching the most."

She was rewarded with a grunt and a look of utter shock that made his eyes turn from crystal to diamond-hard.

With what little dignity she could muster, considering she was dirty and reeking, Jane prissed ahead of him back toward the house.

LENNY WATCHED HER GO, the mad in him wrestling with the sad of his situation. He'd just made a fatal mistake, thinking he could out-dare the little life coach. She'd actually taken him up on that dare. Double-triple-trouble.

"She was right about the pathetic part," he told Boy. Watching the wet, dirty dog bounce and bob around him, he said, "Maybe we both need help."

Female companionship wasn't so bad. Well, unless you married a female just to fill a void in your life. Especially if you married in haste and divorced in a lengthy, well-documented court battle. Three times.

He wouldn't let that happen again, Lenny told himself. This was a little fun with a woman who clearly needed to cut loose and have some fun. And he was the perfect man for that job. He knew how to kick up his heels. He just didn't know how to stay true to one woman. His one flaw, according to the many women who'd stomped out of his life, was not being able to open up and share the angst he carried in his heart. But a man had his pride. Lenny shut down because he couldn't take anyone's pity. He'd seen enough of that growing up and he'd seen it the day he'd lost the big game. And he sure wouldn't open up to this cute little woman who wanted to analyze him and dissect him. No, sir. So he'd have a little fun, put on a good act. And do his best to drive her away. Why change his reputation now?

"So, Boy," he said to his faithful, uncomplicated dog. "How 'bout we let the little life coach unclutter us while we teach her all about throwing caution to the wind?"

Boy's bark indicated it was a solid plan. Lenny wasn't so sure. He might get cured or this little exercise could drive him even deeper into seclusion.

AN HOUR LATER, Jane sat waiting for Lenny to come back from practice but she hadn't wasted her time. She'd gone into a work-related blitz, making more notes and jotting down a list of things she wanted to go over with him. Earlier, after taking a water hose to the worst of the gunk plastered on her borrowed shirt and her dirty shoes, she'd finally managed to get upstairs to take a hot bath in the old-fashioned claw-foot tub in the bathroom next to the frilly bedroom. And realized this was probably the only room in the house that was neat and clean.

The room wasn't very big, but the soft mattress on the four-poster bed seemed to float like a flying carpet each time she sank down on the yellow chenille bedspread. The pillows were covered in lacy white cases embroidered with dainty yellow roses and ribbons. The room smelled of sunshine and fresh air. A high-backed chair with a cane seat sat in one corner near a beautiful ornate armoire. A tall white bookcase brimming with all sorts of literature bespoke someone who loved reading. All the classics were there—from *Little Women* to *Pride and Prejudice* to the Brontë sisters and Flannery O'Connor, as well as several bestselling women's fiction books. And displayed all over the room on every available tabletop and armoire were beautiful porcelain dolls of all shapes and sizes. Someone certainly was a hopeless romantic.

Or had been. Bertie?

Marcus had told her about Lenny's grandmother. Bertie had died of Alzheimer's in February, a week after the Super Bowl game. The game Lenny and his team had lost.

That's all she knew at this point. Lenny valued his privacy a lot more than he seemed to value his public image. Or maybe he had just valued his grandmother's privacy.

Thinking about Bertie's influence over this house and her grandson, Jane tried to imagine Lenny running through the halls of this dainty, overstuffed cupcake of a house. Wondering if Lenny actually ever read anything other than the sports section of the paper and the back of cereal boxes, Jane shook her head.

"Can't wrap my brain around that one," she said as she got dressed in khaki pants and a blue cashmere sweater.

But she did need to wrap her brain around why Lenny was living here in seclusion. He'd spent a lot of time here growing up, so this place had to have a special meaning to him. Obviously, he'd taken his retirement seriously, even if his goofy, hyped-up agent and the rest of the sports world hadn't.

Then she thought about Bertie and the memories Lenny must hold for her and his grandfather. Memories he wasn't willing to let go of. While it was natural to mourn a loved one, it wasn't healthy to refuse to touch anything that loved one had left behind. It would be hard to make him see that this place needed to be put back in order so he could get his own life straight, too. Jane knew hoarding usually began with a traumatic event in a person's life. What had happened to Lenny?

He loved his grandmother. Was that why he'd told her he didn't intend to leave, ever? Or could the real reason be so very private and very hurtful that he refused to even discuss it. What had happened to Lenny's parents?

Lenny Paxton had given up on his career and fame to come home to Arkansas and the one place where he felt safe. But why? Had he really lost his confidence? Did he feel useless and used up? And why was it that way with athletes? Why did they seem to think that winning a game was the most important thing in life?

"Oh, Lenny, you can't do it on your own," she whispered, all sorts of thoughts rushing through her head. "You can't heal. Not until you work through this meltdown everyone keeps talking about."

And why had he put her in this room that seemed so sacred and silent and yet so alive with his grandmother's memory. Why?

We made a deal, Jane thought. And she intended to stick to that deal even though she knew he would put her through her paces. But right now, she had work to do before the Warthogs big game two days from now.

Somehow, in spite of Lenny's need to find some solace, Jane had to show him he'd been looking for it in the right place, but in the wrong way. It wouldn't be easy. Because from what she'd seen so far, Lenny Paxton wasn't going to budge. The man had stubborn written all over his handsome face.

Deciding she'd try to get him to talk more when he got home, Jane headed downstairs. It was nearly dark now, and the old house glowed with a golden thread of light that looked like spun silk falling out across the wide hallway. Dust particles moved through the last of the sun's rays, dancing with abandonment in the still, crisp air. The whole house had the illusion of home and hearth, but Jane could also sense a forlorn kind of sadness floating through those sun rays, too. The house, probably much like the woman who'd once lived here, was trying valiantly to remain prim and proper in spite of certain deterioration.

And her grandson was trying to salvage the memories and the comfort of her love to fill a void in his heart.

She could make this place shine, Jane thought. And she could help Lenny decide what he wanted. Then she remembered falling into his arms in the mud, a delicious shiver radiating throughout her body. Such eyes the man had. No wonder supermodels and housewives alike fell all over him. And in spite of the reports that he'd grown complacent and out of shape, Jane remembered nothing but hard, sinewy muscles and a sense of strength that took her breath away. Which was silly, of course. She wasn't one to get all fluttery and breathless around men. Maybe because she didn't take the time to be around men unless they were in crisis. She didn't date clients, so that was that.

But when she heard Lenny's truck growling up the drive, she did a save of all her notes and tidied up her work space, anxious to talk to him. Her phone vibrated against the oak dresser.

Bryan Culver. The editor of *Sidelined* magazine.

Jane's guilt made her freeze on the spot. She wasn't ready to give Bryan a report yet. She couldn't send anything to the magazine until she had Lennie's complete trust and willingness.

She found him sitting with Boy out in the backyard near a small creek. Taking in the sweet picture, Jane gained a new appreciation for Lenny Paxton. He might be considered a mean, burned-out jock in all the sports and entertainment tabloids, but right now he looked content in his own skin. Lenny laughed and talked as he stroked Boy's furry back, and for just a few seconds, he looked young and carefree again.

Then he looked up and saw her and the wall came back up. Fast and solid.

Taming her beating pulse, Jane made her way down the back steps, noting the hanging baskets of geraniums and ferns surrounding the wraparound porch. The plants looked a lot better than the rest of the house. "Hello," she called, waving. "I hope you had a good practice."

Lenny's smile froze on his face. He willed himself to shut down. He wasn't ready for this woman to see his emotions. Even though they'd laughed about falling in the mud, he'd been silent on the walk back to the house. He'd thought making her barter to stay would scare her away. But Jane had seen enough to figure things out. He needed her—she knew it and he was beginning to see it. It didn't help that he understood her motives even if he didn't welcome her technique.

He stood, taking in her pretty sweater and capri pants. "You clean up real nice, Coach."

"Thanks. So tell me about the Warthogs."

"It's just little boys chasing a football," he said on a grin, wondering why his mood seemed to shift with her around. Maybe because she was so different from most of the women he knew. Her hair, clean and down around her shoulders now, shimmered like the changing leaves, all golden strawberry-blond. Her eyes changed, too, from gold to hazel to brown. This woman was intelligent and studious, no-nonsense and determined, traits he used to possess on the football field.

Traits he had to admire in spite of his resentment toward her. And to fuel that resentment, he couldn't help but play with her. "You know, you don't have to go to the game. Since you hate football."

She grinned then walked ahead of him, her cute hips swaying. "I'm ready to get on with things, including football. Hope you can keep up."

He grabbed her arm. "If that's a challenge, honey, I'm up for the job." He hoped.

She smiled at him again, but didn't look so self-assured now. "Glad to hear that."

Lenny had to wonder why she seemed so content when, in spite of his bravado, doom echoed inside his foggy brain. He'd treated her badly, made her slop pigs, literally dragged her through the mud, even put the moves on her…and still she'd managed to keep that indomitable optimism intact.

And this was just their first day together.

He looked down at Boy. "Good Lord, what have I gotten myself into?"

The big dog barked loud and long. And Lenny could have sworn that dog was grinning.

CHAPTER FOUR

A FEW DAYS LATER, Jane got up at six o'clock, intent on rousting Lenny out for their scheduled early morning jog. If she could get his body back in top form, maybe his mind would soon follow. So she had a workable schedule mapped out and they'd gone for a couple of good, cleansing runs.

Quiet runs. The man didn't talk early in the morning. But she gave him credit for trying. The runs had happened by accident when they'd both shown up in the front yard early one morning. Lenny hadn't said anything. He'd just nodded and grunted then motioned for her to come on.

Today she'd add in some sprints, and strength training, and maybe a little yoga, too. Then they'd tackle the house. Lenny had allowed her to stay but he wasn't too keen on cleaning up around here.

Some deal they had. He mostly either ignored her or grunted at her. And the clock was running toward her deadline of giving *Sidelined* a rough draft of her story. The magazine's hyper editor had left her several pointed voice mails even though she'd stressed to Bryan Culver that she wouldn't write a detailed article about Lenny's "makeover" unless Lenny approved it.

Which he hadn't yet, because she hadn't found the right time to bring up that particular matter.

First she had to convince Lenny to let her start on clearing the kitchen. That could force him to open up and talk to her at least. So, fresh-faced, dressed in black leggings and a supportive blue tank top, and completely limber after a series of yoga and Pilate's stretches, she tied up her ergonomically sound Nikes and bounced downstairs.

Only to find Henry Powell sitting at the breakfast table, sipping coffee.

"Mornin'," he said, never taking his eyes off the worn black book he was reading.

The half light of dawn washed the kitchen in muted grays and whites. "Uh, hi, Henry. Where's Lenny?"

"Gone fishin'."

"Fishing?" Jane headed to the refrigerator.

"Are you deaf?" Henry looked up with brown, doleful eyes.

"No, I'm just…surprised. He could have left me a note maybe. We were supposed to get in a run."

Henry regarded her with a silent look. "He's taking the morning off. And your car is ready. Just get Lenny to drive you to the garage in town."

"Thanks. If Lenny has his way, that could be soon. So what are you doing here?" she asked, thinking she could pump Henry for information.

"I watch the place and do odd jobs. And Lenny said you sure are an odd job."

"Oh." Jane found a mug—this one said Kiss the Cook. "So you help out some?"

"Yep. Lenny likes someone watching so crazy fans and determined reporters don't come in. He especially hates people from corporations sending lawyers down here to remind him of his obligations." He shrugged his bony shoulders. "I'm surprised he didn't at least shoot in the air when I dropped you off."

"He let me live for some reason," Jane replied, learning that being droll went with the territory. She hadn't slept. She'd dwelled too much on the infuriatingly handsome client who seemed to take flirting to a new art form. What *would* he do if he found out she was putting together an article?

She'd tried to bring it up several times, but Lenny's mindset varied from playful and flirty to moody and mean.

Besides, she needed more information and more time.

Taking a sip of her coffee, she evaluated the old man sitting in front of her. Henry Powell was as lanky as a reed pole and just as straight-backed. He wore the required uniform of an Arkansas farmer—faded overalls and plaid button-up shirt, with sturdy brogans on his feet. He was almost bald, except for the few thin strips of gray and brown-tinged hair pulled across the top of his shining head.

"That's very nice of you to help Lenny."

Henry put a finger on the page he'd been reading. "Lenny's mad at me right now because I *did* drop you at his door."

Jane took that into consideration. "Why did you do it if you knew Lenny would be mad?"

He gave her another long, quiet stare.

Glancing down at the book, Jane noticed the title—*The Selected Poems of Emily Dickinson*. "Hmm."

"I used to read this to Bertie." He tapped a long finger on the closed book. "One of her favorites."

"Oh, that was thoughtful." Jane smiled over at him. "So you enjoyed reading this to Bertie?"

"Well, yes, since I love her."

"You love Emily Dickinson. Who doesn't?"

Henry lowered his head and frowned. "Deaf and daft, too."

Jane almost choked on her coffee. "Henry Powell, I can hear perfectly well, thank you. I have a Ph.D. in psychology, so I'm not exactly daft."

"So you said when I gave you a lift."

"Then you'll also remember I'm a life coach."

"Then why don't you get things?"

Confused and anxious to start her day, Jane plopped down in a chair and tore the wrapper off her power bar. "What are you trying to tell me, Henry?"

Henry eyed her chewy protein bar with disdain then leaned across the table to speak in a concise tone, as if he were trying to communicate with a five-year-old. "I loved *Bertie*."

Jane patted him on his gnarled hand. "It sounds as if everyone loved Bertie."

Henry shook his head then opened his volume of poetry.

Baffled, Jane got up to search for some fruit. "Am I missing something here?"

"Yep."

"And are you going to explain it to me?"

"Maybe."

Peeling a banana, she said, "Well, go ahead."

"You're the coach," Henry said, his smile soft and full of a patronizing smirk. "You tell me."

Jane tugged at her tight ponytail. "Tell you what?"

"You ain't used to such as us, are you?"

She chewed the tasty oats, almonds and flaxseed of her breakfast bar. "I'm not, and that's a fact."

"Well, we like just the facts around here. Straight talk, if you get my drift."

She eyed Henry with a new respect. He *was* a straight talker even if he didn't make sense. Not like some men. One man, somewhere nearby at a fishing hole, came to mind.

"We'll grow on you."

"I don't doubt that," she said, getting up to throw her power bar wrapper in the trash. "I'd like to stick around long enough to help Lenny get this place and his life back into tip-top condition."

"He's stubborn."

"I've noticed that. But I can deal with Lenny Paxton. I'm a behaviorist. I like to observe my subjects and then work with them to modify their destructive behaviors."

"Well, it is almost huntin' season."

"Excuse me?"

"You mess with people's minds."

"Not necessarily," she said, waving her half-eaten banana in the air. "I try to help people make lifestyle decisions."

"Like I said, you mess with people's minds."

Jane gave up trying to convince Henry that her motives were pure. Finishing off her meal, she decided she'd find Lenny.

"You're doing it again," Henry said, back to reading his book now.

Chewing, she asked, "Doing what?"

"Thinking too hard. That'll warp your brain."

Jane laughed out loud. "Henry, you amaze me."

"I am pretty amazing."

Seeing his grin, she grinned back at him. "So what's your story, anyway?"

His bushy brows stuck straight up. "You ain't gonna analyze me, now are you, Coach?"

"No, but I'd like to get to know you. I'm just curious."

Henry stopped reading then sank back against his chair. "I was born right here in Mockingbird Springs, in the same house in which my daddy before me was born. I married a girl I'd known since birth and we had five children—lost one son in the Vietnam War, lost a daughter to a car crash out on I-30. The others are married and scattered from hither to yon. My wife died five years ago, in her sleep. And after that, I loved Bertie."

"You loved Bertie." It was a statement. Jane thought back over the conversation and realized what Henry had been trying to tell her. He'd dropped her off here to help Lenny because Henry had loved Bertie. Did that mean she had Henry's blessings?

Jane sat there in the muted light of dawn, and realized this man had lived a full and rich life, right here in a tiny Arkansas town, with the world spinning around him, with tragedy and joy and hard work filling his sunrises and his sunsets. She looked at Henry's long, slender hands and wondered what kind of work those aged, calloused hands had seen, what other hands Henry had held in his. A wife, children, friends, family, faith. Hands to hold. And now, this kind old man was sitting here, reading poetry and watching out for a friend.

Jane looked at her own hands and wondered why she'd never taken the time to have her nails done at a spa, wondered why her fingers looked so weak and frail. When she glanced back up at Henry, he was reading his book again, his face as solemn and shining as the sun rising out over the mountains to the east.

"You loved Bertie. You cared about her."

"Bingo. And I care about her grandson, too."

Jane hoped to get some insight into the woman who'd left such a sweet spirit in this house. "How long did you…love her?"

"Since the day I found her skinny-dipping down in the pond."

"When you were younger?"

"Nope…a couple of years ago." He looked up then. "It wasn't the physical thing, although she was plum cute soaking wet." He shrugged. "But she looked up at me and I knew she needed me. She'd forgotten she wasn't a teenager anymore. I wrapped her in my shirt and got her home and never told a soul, not even Lenny. And since you're a shrink and I just confessed this to you, I'd appreciate it if you treated this like a professional session. You know, confidentiality and all that. I won't have Bertie's memory tarnished by scandal."

Jane leaned toward him, awe and admiration coloring her words. "It will never leave this room."

"Good. 'Cause I don't want Lenny embarrassed or upset. He's tried real hard to protect his privacy and his grandmother's dignity. And I'm trying to abide by his wishes, even if I did leave you at his door."

Then he quoted: "'When night is almost done, And sunrise grows so near, That we can touch the spaces, It's time to smooth the hair.' Bertie loved that particular passage."

Jane swallowed the sweet tears tightening her throat muscles. "I think any woman would love that passage."

Henry nodded, pleased. "Get on now and find Lenny."

Henry wanted her to help his friend. Getting Lenny to cooperate would be hard. But now at least, she had Henry and Emily Dickinson in her corner.

HAVING LENNY IN HER CORNER would be even better, Jane thought as she walked toward the pond on the back of the property. Taking long, stretching strides, she inhaled the crisp dew-kissed morning. Birds were chirping with all the urgency of an alarm clock as they fluttered and flapped around in the tall pines and puffy, gold-leafed oaks. A mockingbird sang out several warbling calls, making Jane wonder if that's how this place had gotten its name.

A fine mist of fog lifted out over the pond, its fingers curling in an invitation as Jane rounded the bend.

She spotted Lenny sitting on the old dock on the other side of the water, watching his cork. He seemed so still and so calm, he almost blended in with the countryside. As she grew closer, however, the sound of Steve Miller's "The Joker" playing low from a boom box hit the air and drowned out the nearby chirping birds. Boy spotted her and came bouncing.

Where had that big dog been hiding anyway? And what was the deal with Steve Miller songs?

"Hello," she called, giving Lenny her best smile while she waylaid Boy, patting his head before he could knock her back with a wet-legged doggy hug. "Hello, Boy. Good dog. Now go away."

The dog greeted her with a tongue-wagging grin; the man greeted her with a scowl. "And here it was so very peaceful and quiet."

"Sorry to disturb you." She walked onto the rickety dock, Boy tracing her steps. "What about our schedule?"

He looked down at his cork. "I'm taking today off."

Ignoring that, she continued. "I thought we could get in a workout along with our daily jogs. You know, sprints, intensity training, power-lifting. I saw your weights out on the porch."

Arching his eyebrows, he gave her a sideways glance. "You're trying to kill me, right?"

"No, I'm trying to get you healthy again." Wanting to remind him of their so-called agreement, she added, "And you can do your coaching thing. Whatever you had in mind."

He scratched his head then slanted another gaze toward her, his eyes the color of the wide-open sky. "Oh, you mean my little deal?"

Jane settled down beside him then pushed Boy out of her face, ignoring the way those vivid blue eyes made her all warm and cold at the same time. "I told you I'll play along. Since you forced me to agree, here I am."

"I don't have to force women to be around me, Coach." Yanking his cork, he growled, "I lost that fish because of you."

"Maybe the fish outsmarted you."

He pulled a squirming worm out of a paper cup and

proceeded to torture it onto the hook. "I'm not so sure about our little deal." He sent her a wink. "No need to tamper with what works."

"But is it working?" She waited a beat, doing some adjusting of her own. "I mean, how long can you rely on Henry to be your bodyguard and patrol?"

Tossing his line out, he said, "Henry helps out because he needs to feel needed. So he'll be around for as long as I'm here. Which, by the way, will be the rest of my I'm-retired-now-so-leave me-alone life."

"Are you allowing Henry to hang around so he can be close to Bertie's things, same as you?"

Aggravation blushed across his features, turning him mean. "I'm not allowing anything. Henry and I go way back. He was there during the worst of it with Bertie. He's as good as gold. I trust him."

Jane decided to open a new dialogue. "He was obviously devoted to Bertie."

"See, we're all very well-adjusted here."

Okay, so that hadn't worked. She had to wonder why he'd clammed up again when things had been moving along. So she pushed. "And how often do you go fishing, or even into town for supplies? When was the last time you had a date? Hiding away here in a disorganized house doesn't make you well-adjusted."

"You ask way too many questions."

"It's part of my job."

"Except that I fired you. And you won't leave."

"No, you offered me a deal and we shook on it, sorta. Now it's pro bono."

"No, more like pro bonehead."

"You don't have to make snide remarks."

"I haven't even begun to make the remarks I'm thinking."

"Could you just answer the questions?"

He shot her a quicksilver grin then leaned so close she could smell the crisp morning air mixed with his aftershave. Was she getting mixed signals or did the man really seem to like her just a little bit? "Okay, dating has never been a problem. I'm going to move that one up on *my* list. Way up." His eyes went a deep misty color that matched the fog. "My list of how to make my little life coach lighten up. When was the last time *you* had a real date?"

The way he said that implied that Jane hadn't had a whole lot of anything lately. And there went that delightful anticipation sliding down her spine.

"I'm not interested in dating you, Lenny," she said, even though her mind played with that idea much in the same way Boy was playing with some frayed rope, chewing on it and groping at it.

"Ah, now, don't disappoint me," he said as he lifted his line and readjusted it. "I can be pretty persuasive when I want to, Coach."

She swallowed, her mind imagining all the ways he could be persuasive. Was this another one of his games? Lure her out here then play hard to get, followed by flirting? She cleared her throat and her head. "So women just naturally come to you?"

"Something like that. One of my exes lives about a half mile from here. I see her on a regular basis. One lives in Texas, just a stone's throw away. The other one kind of comes and goes, but she's always around when I need her."

Good grief, the man hoarded more than football equipment and his grandmother's doll collection. "So you rely on your ex-wives to keep you company?"

"They seem to like my company." He shrugged, his broad shoulder flexing underneath his shirt. "And who am I to send them away. I still like all of 'em, even if I can't live with any of 'em."

It was a cool morning, but Jane felt a soft sheen of sweat popping out on her brow. Lenny had a lot of issues about letting go. "Don't you think that's kind of pathetic? Stringing them along like that?"

"I don't have to string anything along, suga'. Except this stubborn fish." He pulled the line again, grunting when it came up minus the worm. "You are bad luck."

"Sorry. Let's get back to your so-called love life."

"Curious, huh?"

She ignored his broad grin, afraid he'd realize he was actually answering personal questions. "I need to understand all the dynamics, yes."

"Uh-huh." He fixed another doomed worm onto his hook. "There were a whole lot of dynamics in each marriage, let me tell you."

"Go ahead then," she said with a determined dare, figuring this was another of his tricks. "Tell me. I mean, besides ex-wives, do you also have other women hanging around?"

"Apparently. *You're* still here, aren't you?"

Jane pushed her palms against the cool wood of the deck. "I'm...never mind. Give me some examples of the kind of women you keep around." This would be good fodder for her article.

He frowned but nodded. "Well, let's see. There's Wanda. She has a nice salon in town."

"A hairdresser?"

"A beautician," he corrected. Then he glanced at his watch. "And she's due here this morning." Laughing, he shook his fishing line. "I always enjoy Wanda's visits."

"Why is Wanda coming to your house?" Maybe she didn't want to know the answer to that particular question, Jane thought too late.

"She trims my hair. I don't like to go into town, so she drives out here. She does this neck massage thing, too." He smiled sweetly. "Real nice. Wanda has a gift."

Jane could guess the implications of that husky-throated compliment and drat, if she didn't also imagine giving him a neck massage herself. "So even though you can't wait to get rid of *me*, you're excited about seeing Wanda."

"Wanda isn't a nag. I think she'd like to be my fourth wife."

Squirming right along with his worms, Jane said, "Why don't you look at this differently. Wanda is coming here to help out. Henry is here to help out. I'm here to help out. You obviously need other people in your life but for some reason you've got all of us catering to you. And that's the problem, I think. Simple, right?"

Touchdown, Jane.

He put his pole down then grabbed the thermos sitting beside him on the dock. Giving her a long look that had her shivering again in the cool morning breeze, he poured himself a cup of steaming coffee. "Coach, I have a very bad feeling that anything involving you definitely won't be simple." Then he toasted her with the cup before taking a sip of the coffee.

The gravelly sweetness of his early-morning voice slid over her like sap sliding down a pine tree. "Why am I any different from everyone else who's trying to help you?" she asked, proud that her words didn't quiver the way her insides seemed to be doing.

He tossed back the rest of his coffee. "You came with stipulations and schedules. You came highly recommended and probably overpaid by my moron of an agent. You came uninvited and unwanted. And you're still here, willing to try this without pay, even after I cooked up that let's-make-a-deal arrangement and humored you. I'd say that makes you pretty complicated. Not to mention, a regular nuisance."

Jane got up to stare down at him, her hands on her hips. "I am not all that complicated, and I'm not trying to be a nuisance. And after evaluating this situation, I truly think you're using all the clutter around you as a shield. So if you thought making that deal with me and pacifying me for a few days would get me to leave, well, you thought wrong. A deal is a deal."

Because he'd pushed her too far, she went headlong into her interrogation. "So when are you going to actually do your part? When are you going to show me the Lenny Paxton Plan for spicing up my life?"

Right now, it seemed. He stood up, dropped his pole and tugged her close. Jane's shivers turned into a pool of liquid heat as his eyes roamed her face with predatory interest. She honestly thought he was going to kiss her. If he didn't kill her.

"I let you stay just for fun," he said, dropping his hands. "Like you said, a deal is a deal. I kept my end of the bargain and now I want you to end this silliness right now by doing both of us a favor. Leave gracefully, okay?"

Frustrated and flustered, she took a step backward. "You call that a bargain? You didn't mean any of it, did you, Lenny? Why are you too stubborn to see—"

"Stop," he said, pushing her away. "All deals are off. I was teasing you and flirting with you, but I've changed my mind. You aren't my type, anyway."

Jane held a finger in his face, but backed up even more because he was too overwhelmingly close. "I will not stop. I'm willing to give you some pointers, whether you pay me or not, and whether you think you need them or not."

And really, whether she wrote an article about it or not, she realized. "Just listen to me—"

He reached out, holding a hand up in her face as he inched closer. "I said stop."

But Jane didn't want to stop and she really didn't want him to get any closer. That is until she felt the edge of the dock hitting against her Nikes. But by then, it was too late. She started wobbling like the red-and-white cork floating out in the water, and the next thing she felt was air. Struggling to stay balanced, she saw Lenny's hand flying out toward her. But it was too late for that, too.

"I told you to stop," he shouted as she fell off the dock and hit the water.

The last thing she saw before she went under was the big grin on his face. Followed by a look of pure concern. Then she felt the cold water surrounding her. Jane was a good swimmer, but the chilly water gripped her, weighing her down until a strong arm grabbed her.

LENNY LET OUT A CURSE then took off his boots and dove in after Jane, his mind whirling with all the reasons he'd woken up this morning determined to end this little charade. Number one being he had a thing for the life coach. A real annoying thing that caused him to dream sweet dreams and wake up in a deep sweat and a really bad mood.

His deal had backfired on him, big time.

And now, his life coach was sinking like a lead weight and well, he couldn't let the woman drown. He saw her trying to surface, grabbed her and pulled her up, holding her as they both treaded water.

"You pushed me in the pond," she said through a sputter, water cascading off her whole body.

"You fell in," he countered.

"You thought it was funny."

He hauled her up onto the dock then pulled himself up beside her, rivulets of water dripping all around them. "I didn't think it was funny. Am I laughing?"

He wasn't. This just wasn't fun anymore.

"You look mad," she said on a breathless rush. "I don't get why you're so mad, Lenny."

And she looked good, sitting there all wet and wild. Which made him not so very mad anymore. The woman was good at her job. She was in his head, going deep. "I can't explain it," he admitted. "You're not like any other woman I've ever been around." Lenny knew what was bothering him. He *wanted* to open up this woman. He *wanted* to tell her all about his pain and his inability to put one foot in front of the other most days.

For a minute, their eyes met and everything went still. The autumn air sizzled with a heated rush.

Then because he was in such a fix, Lenny started laughing.

Which made Jane extremely mad. Even soaking wet, she did a really good job of showing him just how mad.

"Do you keep putting me in these situations so that I'll give up and leave?"

He wiped at his eyes, but dropped the smile. "Yeah, something like that."

"And here I thought you were going to show me the real Lenny Paxton. You know what I think?"

"No, but I'm sure you're gonna tell me."

"I think the real Lenny Paxton is hiding away here because he's afraid to face the world. I think you've lost your drive and your confidence and I think you need to work through your home's clutter as well as all that emotional clutter in your big, thick skull."

His jolly mood turned to molten blue haze. "And you're the woman to help me do it, right?"

"Exactly."

Exactly. And that was the problem.

"You're on," he said, pushing a hand over his wet hair. "Starting right now." Then he grabbed her and, full of dare and danger, he kissed her, good and proper.

CHAPTER FIVE

JANE TUGGED AWAY from all that heat, the imprint of his lips on hers sizzling away the wet chill. "It's my turn to tell you to stop. *That* is not part of the deal."

"Oh, yes it is," he said, his eyes glistening with triumph. "It's part of *my* deal. Didn't I make that clear?"

"But it's not…allowed," Jane retorted, her mouth still warm, her pulse dancing like the ripples on the water.

He yanked her back into his arms, his strength reminding her of all the walls she was trying to break down, his eyes reminding her of his macho-induced charm. "Oh, I think it is allowed—that's the best part. I have to live up to my womanizing repetition, don't I? I tried to warn you." Standing her back up straight, he watched as water poured down her shivering body, then glanced at his bobbing cork. "I reckon I'll never see that particular fish again."

Jane sputtered, spewing water away from her face and hair. "I fall in the lake, you kiss me and you're worried about your fish? Your issues are far worse than I thought."

He brushed at her wet velour jacket, then turned and grabbed a windbreaker from the deck. Draping it around her shivering shoulders, he said, "Yeah. I wanted fish for lunch."

Boy came up, sniffing at her, his expression full of wonder on why he hadn't been in on the fun. He let loose with a few little half barks to clarify his point.

"Oh, get away from me, both of you," Jane shouted, pushing through the man-dog team blocking her way. "I'll have to go change." Then she turned to face the still smiling Lenny Paxton. "But I'm not done here, Lenny. Oh, no. You think you can tease me, pick at me and push me in the lake?"

"Hey, I did not push you in the lake. You fell. And don't forget the part about where I kissed you. I kinda liked that part. And you didn't try to stop me. In fact, you kinda kissed me back."

Dragging a hand through her hair, she yelled, "Well, only because you got right in my face, when I fell in and when you kissed me."

"That's how kissing happens, in case you've never tried it—"

"I know what you thought you were doing, but did you have to try to seduce me right away? That's way too close for our working relationship, Lenny."

He stepped around Boy. The dog's ear perked up at this new development, causing him to let out another bark of appreciation for whatever new game they were about to play.

"Oh, you mean this close?" Lenny said, grabbing her by the arms as he leaned inches from her face, his expression blazing like the bright early morning sun. "Is this too close?"

Jane thought she might hyperventilate. She could see the crystal flecks in his eyes, could see the dare, the challenge of his intensely soft smile.

"You don't like being this close to me? Is that it?"

"Yes, that's it," she said. "I need breathing room. I'm…I'm not a toucher. I don't…touch people. So just back off, please?"

He let her go, waiting as she scurried away. Then he said, "Well, that's exactly how you're making me feel. Closed in and stifled, as if I can't breathe."

That stopped her cold. So she was getting to the man, after all. His admission certainly changed the game plan.

Flabbergasted, Jane advanced on him, but not nearly as close as he'd been with her. But she had to keep drawing him out of that football-helmet shell. "You can't possibly make that kind of comparison. I want to help you, not hem you in. Why is that so hard for you to accept?"

"It's not hard—I just don't need you here. And I like my women to be touchy-feely. Where's the fun in a no-touching rule?"

His words hit her with all the force of the chilly water. He didn't need her here and she did have a problem with showing her own emotions. On a professional level, she knew he was in denial and that he'd do or say anything to keep that denial intact, even something such as pushing her to her limits. But on a personal level, that remark cut like a piece of rusty barb wire. Since she'd tried every tactic in the book with him and some that weren't even *in* the book, Jane felt a sweeping defeat. She was supposed to cure his problems and yet he'd managed to zoom in on one of her biggest insecurities. Why couldn't she ever relax and enjoy being with men instead of analyzing them?

Lenny watched her, his eyes moving over her face. "Do you get it now?"

"Oh, yes, I get it," she said. With a shuddering breath, she waved her hands in the air. "I was wrong—on so many levels." With that she turned to stomp back up the rickety pier toward the shore, Boy hot on her heels. And while she stomped, she tried to ignore the shame of this defeat.

"Coach, wait a minute." She heard a harsh intake of breath, then, "Jane, would you just come back here?"

The dog turned to give the man a questioning look. But even though she considered it a breakthrough moment that he'd actually called her by her given name with a pleading tone, the woman kept right on walking, each squish of water inside her Nikes reminding her that she was about to do something she'd never done before. Give up.

LENNY BEAT HER back to the house. He knew the short-cut. And he could still outrun a jackrabbit, even if the world and everyone in it thought he was a has-been.

Why was it that no one ever stopped to think how insulting that particular label could be to a man who'd worked hard all his life to do his best?

He ran fast because he was so mad, hitting the side of the sloping yard with a skid that didn't really help his protesting knees or his rickety back. But he didn't want the life coach to leave angry. In fact, he didn't want her to leave at all. Which only aggravated him all the more. "Oh, just great."

Wanda Lawhorn's yellow Thunderbird sat perched on his front drive. He wished he'd canceled their appointment—or *date* as Wanda liked to call it. "Another one to deal with."

Some days even a man who truly loved women just needed to get away from the whole female pack.

"But not today," he thought, quoting a character from the movie *Gladiator*. "Not yet, not yet."

He made it into the kitchen just in time to find Wanda laying out her equipment—scissors and combs. He worried mostly about the scissors. Especially when Wanda got wind of the little life coach hot on his trail. Wanda looked up as he made a loud entry, her smile apple-pie pretty. "Hey, suga'. I'm ready."

His breath hitching in his stomach, Lenny nodded then bent double to rest his lungs. "You didn't have to come today, Wanda. I know how busy you are." Not knowing what else to say, he headed for the water jug.

Wanda put a hand on her denim-and-diamonds-clad

hip then popped her Wrigley's gum. "I sure hope that old bear looks worse than you do."

"What?" Lenny asked, his back to her, the scent of Final Net and Breck lingering in the air all around him in spite of the sweat he'd worked up on his run. Or his escape, depending on how a man looked at things.

Wanda sashayed over to lean on the counter, her low-cut sequined sweater stretching across her voluptuous figure. "You look like you been wrestling a mean old bear. It's dangerous in them woods out there, I reckon."

Lenny turned to stare over at her. "I was exercising."

"Yep, and with your jeans on. That must have hurt, tight as they are." Her gaze slid down his body, her smile full of feminine delight. "How'd you get all wet?"

"I just—" He was about to explain things to her, and warn her to please not mess with the woman he heard stomping up the back steps, but it was too late.

Like a cat sniffing for a mouse, Wanda's nostrils flared as Jane entered the room. The beautician came up off the counter and stood to her full five-foot-four status, her stiletto mules tapping against the floor. "You must be the life coach."

Jane stood in the doorway, her ponytail tangled and dripping with water and wet leaves, her yoga pants clinging and stretched. Wiping at her face, she said, "Excuse me, but I'm just passing through." Giving Lenny a look that could bake biscuits, she added, "I'll be gone in an hour."

Henry ambled into the kitchen with a frown on his face and a hard glare toward Lenny in his eyes.

"You owe me twenty bucks, Henry," Wanda said, holding out her hand. "A bet's a bet. And since she only lasted a few days, I'd say I won fair and square."

"You bet on me?" Jane asked, her tone dignified in spite of the mud spots on her yoga pants.

Wanda gave Jane a sympathetic look then whirled to Lenny. "C'mon, honey, let's get you a nice cup of coffee and a piece of sweet potato pie."

"She didn't bake it," Henry said as he slammed a twenty-dollar bill on the table. "Barbara did."

"It's the thought that counts," Wanda replied with a sultry smile.

Lenny felt trouble all the way down to his arthritic ankles. "I'm not hungry. I'm getting out of these wet clothes."

Wanda refocused her attention on Jane much in the way a cat would stare at a bird. "Honey, did that scoundrel try to drown you?"

Jane looked as if she might answer yes, but Lenny held up a hand to stop her. "It's okay." Then he turned to Jane. "Uh, could I have a word with you?"

"I think we've said everything we had to say," Jane retorted, one of her squishing Nikes tapping against the floor in a battle with Wanda's noisy stilettos.

It didn't take an expert in body language to tell that

she was not in a negotiating mood, but Lenny tried. "Look, I need to discuss some stuff with you."

"Oh, really?" Jane looked at the other woman watching them with gum-smacking intensity. Lifting a hand, and water drops, too, she smirked at him. "Now you want to discuss things? Too late, I'm afraid."

Wanda came around the counter, popping her gum, a grin on her face as she gave Jane a thorough analysis. "Suga', you might be a life coach, but mercy-me, you sure could use a makeover."

Jane didn't speak. She just stood there, a shocked expression on her face, her hands on her hips.

A wiser woman would have left it at that, but Wanda wasn't known for her wisdom. Lenny watched in amazement as she expertly steered the confused, wet, fighting-mad life coach toward her portable beauty station.

"Let's just get you all prettied up. I'm telling you there ain't nothing like a makeover to change a woman's perspective." Then she leaned close. "Nor a man's."

Lenny looked at Wanda's smug, dimpled smile, and knew this situation had just gone from bad to worse. She would give Jane a makeover, all right. But he didn't think the life coach was gonna like it, not one bit.

Boy whimpered and headed back out to the porch, astute animal that he was.

Wanda, however, grinned and clapped her hands. "I can't wait to see the outcome. It'll surprise you, I promise," she said to Jane, the slant of her cat eyes scaring Lenny. "Just you wait and see."

"I don't think—"

"Hush, now," Wanda replied to Jane's protest. "This one's on the house. The House of Wanda, by the way. The official name is Wanda's Wash and Curl. I'm right up on the main highway. Used to be a KFC, but now we serve up more fun stuff instead of chicken wings. I got me a good deal on the building, and well, I've always admired those cute little conelike roofs on the old KFC restaurants."

Waiting for her to take a breath, and completely amazed by her false eyelashes and ruby-red lips, Jane put on the purple terry robe Wanda shoved at her while Wanda nudged her toward the kitchen sink. Looking around for Lenny, Jane saw that he had managed to disappear. Just like the man.

"I don't need—"

"You're gonna love Wanda," Henry said, making himself right at home across from Jane. "She has a way with hair."

"I can see," Jane mumbled just before Wanda pushed her headfirst into the sink. Not that Henry's word counted. He was almost bald. "But I don't—"

"How long you planning on being here?" Wanda asked over the spray of warm water from the sink hose. "You know, everybody's talking about the life coach. It's life coach, this, and life coach, that. I do declare, you'd think we've never heard of a life coach around these parts."

"We haven't," Henry pointed out.

Jane tried to stand up, but Wanda pushed her back down with a remarkably strong hand, managing to soak Jane's already wet hair. "Lenny likes a certain kind of woman, don't you know? And besides, he's retired. He's done with being coached—in anything."

Henry snorted. "Jane is not only good at figuring people out and organizing things. She's also well-read. She reads Emily Dickinson."

Wanda laughed. "If it ain't to do with hair or Hollywood, I don't read it, honey." She winked at Jane. "Know what I mean?"

Jane thought she had it figured out. Trying to relate, she nodded through Wanda's overzealous shampoo massage. "I love all types of publications. I read across the board."

"You do?" Wanda asked, her heavily lined eyes lifting. "I'da never guessed that, what with you being all scholarly and smart. Henry said you're some kind of doctor, right?"

Jane gave in to being tortured, but she let out a sigh as the hot water hit her head. "I have a Ph.D. in psychology, yes."

"That does sound fancy," Wanda replied. "Might be a tad too fancy for some around here."

Jane didn't miss the way she glanced down the hall toward Lenny's room. "I'm here to help," Jane said over the gush of water moving down her head.

"Of course you are, honey." Wanda lifted her up then

plopped a towel on her head. Guiding Jane toward a chair, she said, "Same as me."

"It is nice of you to make house calls," Jane replied, not sure how to extract herself from this situation. She wanted to leave with what little dignity she had left, but she had a gut feeling that notion would be shattered. Maybe she could get some insight out of Wanda at least. "But shouldn't Lenny be able to drive into town?"

"He likes his privacy," Wanda said through her pink bubble as she sprayed a strong-smelling solution on Jane's hair then ripped a wide-toothed comb through it. "And he doesn't like leaving the farm."

Trying again, Jane said, "Have you known him long?"

Wanda turned all dreamy. "I've known Lenny since... mercy, since we were both running around in first grade, I reckon. And Miss Bertie taught me in grammar school and during Sunday school, God rest her soul. I feel like one of the family."

Jane remembered what Lenny had said about Wanda. They certainly must have a close relationship. Maybe that would explain why Wanda was working so hard to pull every hair in Jane's head out by the roots.

But two could play at that game, Jane thought, ignoring her uncomfortable wet clothes. If she went along with this "makeover," maybe she'd be able to get some information out of Wanda (even though she had technically just quit this project). "So tell me about growing up here," she began, hoping Lenny wasn't within earshot.

"Nothing much to tell," Wanda said. "Small town. Same old crowd. Memories, some good and some bad."

Jane heard crinkling and turned to see what looked like little foil wrappers. "What's that?"

"For your highlights," Wanda replied, smiling pretty.

"I don't need—"

"Yes, you do. Trust me."

"I like my hair the way it is."

Wanda made a clucking sound in her throat. "That's because you've never tried it any other way. How long you had this hairdo, anyway?"

Jane thought back. "Uh, since college."

Wanda tapped her comb against the table. "See there? You need a change."

Jane lifted her eyebrows. "I thought coming here would be a change."

"Oh, it is for sure. Big city girl stuck at the bottom of this little mountain. I'm sure you can't wait to get back to Little Rock."

Getting the impression that Wanda couldn't wait for that, either, Jane took another breath, thinking her decision to give up might have been too hasty. "Let's talk some more about you. Are you...married?"

"Not at the moment," Wanda replied over the sound of foil crinkling. "I probably should be doing this on dry hair, but we had to get all that pond scum off your head, now didn't we? How'd you manage to fall in, anyway?"

Before she could stop herself, Jane blurted out, "I was backing away from Lenny."

Wanda went still. "Oh, really? Humph. He does like to be around women. *I* should know."

Okay, that was a definite turf term, if Jane had ever heard one. Hoping to alleviate some of Wanda's paranoia, she said, "I'm here on a strictly professional level. I don't intend to get involved with Lenny. I've heard all about his reputation."

And she'd experienced that reputation, her lips all over his earlier at the pond. The man could kiss, and his famous quarterback hands still had the moves, too.

"Have you now?" Wanda dropped her hands then came around to stare at Jane. "What'd you hear?"

Wondering why Wanda didn't go into interrogation work, Jane shrugged and hoped she looked bored with this whole conversation. "Oh, about the three ex-wives—"

"Not a one of them understands Lenny the way I do."

"And the run-ins with bouncers—"

"He doesn't like being pushed around when he's having fun at a party."

"And his being rude to reporters—"

"They get in his face and make him so mad."

"And—this whole contract situation."

"Two sides to every story," Wanda retorted. "And just where do you get your information, honey?"

Jane stopped there. "I can't divulge my research. That wouldn't be professional."

"I understand," Wanda said, patting her puffy chignon. "I have my own professional standards, too, you know."

"You seem very professional to me," Henry said, his hands folded together on the table as he watched the makeover with deep fascination. "I'm kinda enjoying this."

"I'm certainly having a blast myself," Wanda replied. Then she proceeded to paint some awful-smelling substance on Jane's foiled hair.

"What's that?" Jane asked, straining to look at Wanda.

Henry craned his long red neck. "It's bright green."

Jane squirmed. "I don't want my hair to be a funny color."

Wanda held fast. "It won't be. Just some pretty gold streaks here and there—like the trees turning outside."

"I don't want to look like a tree, either."

Wanda looked affronted. "Didn't I tell you I'm a professional?"

"Yes, you did." Jane sank back, trying not to breathe the ammonia-filled fumes. "When will we be done?"

Wanda lifted Jane out of the chair then turned it toward the space-helmet contraption on the breakfast table. "Oh, in about thirty to forty minutes. We'll use Bertie's old hair dryer, God rest her sweet soul. Can't rush this, or you might for sure come out green."

The next thing Jane knew, she was underneath the bulky space helmet and Wanda had the heat turned to full blast.

With a sweet way that looked innocent, Wanda leaned down close and shouted at Jane. "I'm gonna visit with Lenny for a bit. You stay there until I come back for you, okay, honey?"

Jane nodded, already sweating through her wet clothes and the heavy robe. "But—"

"No thanks necessary," Wanda replied, patting Jane's leg. "My pleasure." Then she moved a long glossy fingernail down to Jane's hands. "It's just a shame I didn't think to bring my manicure set. Your nails look kinda rough around the edges."

Jane watched, helpless, as Wanda whispered something in Henry's ear. Henry got up, gave Jane a sympathetic look then hightailed it for the door. While Jane sat there and fried.

CHAPTER SIX

LENNY DIDN'T WANT to stare. But it was like that train wreck thing. He couldn't look away.

Jane ignored him as she moved her luggage down the stairs, her head held high.

And piled high.

Wanda had done a real number on the life coach. And to his shame and disgrace, he could have stopped it, but he hadn't. And now he sure regretted that. He regretted a lot about this whole affair. Except for that kiss out on the pier. He should regret that, but he didn't.

He liked the way the life coach kissed.

"Jane," he began, not knowing how to approach this subject. "Jane?"

She kept moving toward the front door. "Henry's going to give me a ride to—" Then she stopped and turned around.

"Actually, I'm not quite sure where Henry will take me. I don't know where my car is."

"We'll find your car," Lenny said, trying not to flinch as he got his first good look at the front of her new hairdo and the heavy makeup Wanda had insisted on applying. "Jane—"

She lifted a hand then stared up at him through her kohl-rimmed, smoky-shadowed, heavily mascaraed eyes. "Do not say anything about my hair or my face. I don't want to take the time to wash this *waterproof* stuff off, and I refuse to humiliate myself any further by bursting into tears about my ruined hair. It's just hair. It can be salvaged. Right now, I only want to get out of here." Then she happened to glance in the oval mirror by the hall-side table. With a gasp, she brought a hand up to the too-short, too-red-and-brown-striped fringe of bangs sticking up around her forehead. "Uh, oh—"

Lenny tugged her away from the mirror. "Wanda has a strange sense of humor."

"And an apparent death wish against me," Jane replied, her hand still touching tentatively at her butchered, spiked hair. "Why did I let that woman get her hands on me?"

Lenny pulled her into the parlor. "You were mad and confused and, well, Wanda can be a bit overwhelming at times."

"You think?"

He grinned then turned somber at her murderous look. "I'm sorry about Wanda. If it makes you feel any better, she actually believes she gave you a great makeover."

"Oh, that certainly helps," Jane said, touching a hand to the back of her teased, shagged do. "I don't have much hair left. And what little I do have is now part burgundy and part brass-colored gold."

Lenny leaned forward, hoping to cheer her up. "I kinda like it. Reminds me of Pat Benatar."

"You are so lost in the seventies, aren't you?"

"She was more early eighties, I believe."

"Well, since I remind you of her—go ahead, hit me with your best shot."

Lenny felt bad that Jane seemed defeated. He had almost liked her feisty nature. She'd been so sure of herself...it was, well, kind of a turn-on. But he did want her to leave. Didn't he? He didn't want to be the one to cause her any uncertainty, but he didn't want her here pestering him, either. Wanda had finished what he'd started, freaking out the life coach. But looking at her now, he wasn't so sure he was ready to let her go after all. She was a real pain, but a refreshingly different kind of pain. She'd made him start breathing again.

But she'd also made him see inside himself—and he didn't like what he'd found there.

"I don't know what to say. I'm sorry, I guess."

"You guess? Could you possibly sound any more compassionate and repentant?"

"Hey, I said I'm sorry. Want me to take you to the drugstore in town to get your real hair color back?"

She got up and hurried to the mirror again. With a groan, she ran her hands through her hair. "No, that might make matters worse. And besides, I'm sure everyone in town is having a field day laughing. They all already think I'm a quack, anyway."

Lenny came to stand in the doorway, his hands tucked

into his jean pockets. "Well, now that you've fluffed your interesting hairdo a bit, you make a cute quack."

She sank down on the stairs, her head in her hands. "I wanted to make a difference with you, Lenny. So much that I was willing to allow Wanda to do this so I could get information about *you*." Then she lifted a hand, gesturing. "I mean, look around. This place is cluttered and dusty and a mess. You live in a flea market. I wasn't sure of your agent's motives at first, but after seeing this house I can understand his concern." Then she lifted back up. "I was anxious to change you, but now, well, it's more about organizing this beautiful old house. If you'd just let me."

Lenny followed the line of her flapping hands. She was right, of course. He'd let things go since Bertie's death. Since even before Bertie's death. No wonder Marcus had panicked when he'd come out here with those infernal contracts. The superagent probably thought Lenny was turning into some kind of Howard Hughes recluse.

"I...I don't know what to do," he admitted to Jane.

Early this morning, he'd been all geared up to finish this, to tell her to find the quickest way back to Little Rock. But then he'd kissed her. Then Wanda had done this, and the life coach had turned human on him. In spite of what the world thought of him, Lenny Paxton did have a heart. For reasons he didn't want to explore, this pesky little woman was beginning to grow on him. That spiky, saucy hairdo and her new sultry eyes were driving him a little crazy. Yeah, he had a thing for women, even women who wanted to change him. Many had tried; all so far had failed. Which usually meant costly lawyers and monthly payments to an ex-wife.

Which would explain his lapse in good sense when the next words came out of his mouth.

"Let's go over our options," he said, sprawling down on the stairs, his legs straight out in front of him. "I had a coach back in college, a *real* coach, who always sat us down and said that very thing whenever we were behind in the game. He'd say, 'Boys, let's go over our options. First—we have two—we can either play to win or plan on losing. I want to win. So that's one option.' Then he'd explain about option two—losing. Which really wasn't an option at all."

She listened, nodding. "I don't want to lose, either, but there doesn't seem to be a reason to stay."

"Oh, there *are* other options," he replied, leaning back on his elbows. "I could take you back to Little Rock myself, but that's two hours each way and I don't like long road trips." And he'd be all alone with her in a car, a captive subject for her to dissect and analyze. No way.

She gave him a long look through her sultry new eyes. "Call Henry. He'll probably be thrilled to be known as the man who drove the life coach right out of town. Or at least to my car."

Lenny slanted her a sideways gaze, noticing the pretty flecks of gold in her eyes. "No, I think I'd be the one who'd get that particular label. To add to my many other labels."

She made a face, her cute little nose crinkling. "Okay, then we're back to letting me stay."

"Yep. But I'm still not so sure—"

"I won't try to mess with your head, as Henry so sagely put it. But I will continue clearing out this stuff. You'd have to help me, of course."

He nodded. "That is a good option. A win/win situation. But you're an important person. I'm sure you'd rather go back to your practice in Little Rock. Don't you have some clients who're worse off than me?"

She shook her head, spikes of hair glistening as she moved. "I cleared my calendar to come here."

"That figures." Lenny couldn't understand why she'd felt the need to do that, but then, he figured life coaches had their own set of playbooks. And he also figured Marcus had offered her major bucks to "cure" him.

"We've got a good exercise and diet program started, but you need more organizational skills," she said. "We'll use practical application. I'll study your habits—"

He sat up, all his kind thoughts going out the screen door. "This isn't some weird freak show, doc. And my problem is fairly simple. Most of this stuff belonged to the woman who raised me, so I'm having a hard time getting rid of it."

Jane pushed toward her side of the stairs, her eyes brimming with understanding. "I didn't mean it that way." Then she let out a sigh. "I'm used to speaking in those terms. I meant no disrespect. I'd truly like to counsel you and yes, take notes, make observations, to benefit future clients who might be going through the same thing."

He relaxed, forgiving her for her shrink-speak. "Just so you know, I won't have my grandmother's memory exposed or scrutinized. I want to keep this private, for her sake. That's all I've ever wanted."

She looked down and away. "You should start by explaining that to your agent."

"Are you kidding? Marcus would sell the exclusive to the *National Enquirer* if he thought it would get me back in the limelight. And I don't want to be in the limelight, and I sure don't want to get caught in another frenzy of media hoopla. It shouldn't be this hard for a man to retire." Then he shot her a solemn look. "That's the deal breaker, doc. I gave it all up to come here and rest. Just rest. And I changed my mind about the endorsement deal for my own reasons. Understand?"

"I understand," she said, holding onto a loose stair spindle. But she still looked nervous. "All the more reason to let me teach you how to find peace in your life. I won't mess with the contract dispute, if you'll let me do something with this house. Living in such disarray and clutter can't be healthy."

"I thought I was doing okay on that."

Jane pointed to the long hallway. "You can barely make it to your bedroom, Lenny. How can you decide anything about your life if you can't even throw away old newspapers and magazines or sort and read the mail?"

They sat silent for a couple of minutes, the sound of birds chirping coming through the open door. "There are no other options if you want to get some control over your life again," she finally said. "The deal is—I'll help you get this house organized and cleaned up, and when and if you're ready, I'll do the same for your head. And while I'm here, you can teach me how to…uh…loosen up a bit. But only in a friendly, professional way. None of that Lenny Paxton funny business."

He scrunched his face, thinking. Knowing he'd probably regret this and knowing he'd have to have some funny business in there somewhere or he really would go crazy, he said, "Well, I guess I can live with that. I have some fall crops that need attending—some pumpkins and greens, things like that. I could use the help in my garden—that'll be your first lesson from me."

"I can do that. Then we'll start you on getting the mail sorted out and work on this house—room by room." She gave him the once-over. "And you need to continue the exercise and the new diet."

Lenny said something that surprised even him, only because he'd decided he liked her. "I *might* need you, after all. But only if we stick to the original deal. Is there a way we can do this together and maybe have a little fun in the process?"

She put her elbows on her knees, her hands up. Then she put her head in her hands. "I remember fun."

"So do we have a deal or not? A real deal this time. And it might mean you'll start to love football, just warning you."

Then she raised her head and looked him straight in the eye. "I can handle football if you can handle getting down to the tough issues. Do *you* want this deal?"

Lenny had to swallow the solid fear lodging inside his heart. Those eyes of hers reminded him of the sweet glow of a beautiful fall sunset—etched with shining colors of light. He wanted to keep her around for a little while longer.

"Deal." He took her hand in his, shaking it, then holding it, his fingers loving the softness of her touch. "Deal. I want you to stay."

There, he'd said it, and already he regretted it. But he'd regret letting her leave all mad and all made-up even more. Or maybe this felt so much like his last game, the one where he was supposed to have carried his team to a victory. The one where his shoulder had twisted into a knot of pain and he'd heard something snap and he'd made a bad throw. The one where the ball had been intercepted by the fastest running back on the other team. Yeah, that game.

Maybe he didn't want this to end in such an ugly way, which would make him the big loser again, the way he'd been labeled on all the sports pages. "Jane?"

She lifted up, staring at him through the fringe of those ridiculous bangs. "It's a deal."

She smiled so brightly, Lenny had to grab a spindle

himself. He really wished she'd quit going all cute on him. "Now don't go getting any notions. I didn't say you could stay forever."

"I know you didn't, but this is a start."

She hopped up, her cropped little corduroy breeches swishing as she moved. "Oh, there's Henry. Want to tell him we don't need him after all?"

Lenny went to the screen door. "I'll invite him in for some more coffee and pie, to soften the blow."

"We still have pie left?"

"Yep. Sweet potato."

"Did you cook it?"

"No. Wanda brought it, but Barbara cooked it. It's not healthy, but sweet potatoes are good for the soul."

"Who's Barbara?"

"My second ex-wife. She lives at the other end of the property."

"Is she as devious as Wanda?"

"No. She's sweet and quiet, and she makes good pie."

"In that case, I happen to love sweet potato pie."

"Grab us some plates, then."

Lenny watched as she hurried off to do that, then he turned to find Henry standing on the steps staring at him.

"Well, is she staying or going?" Henry asked, his hands hanging on his suspenders. "I've wasted half the day watching this soap opera but I had to leave before the grand finale. This beats *All My Children* hands down."

"Staying for now," Lenny replied. "You might want to get that twenty back from Wanda."

Henry rocked back on his brogans, grinning. "Now that's a strange turn of events, considering all the talk in town. I was the only one who thought she'd last a day."

"You should know better than to listen to talk."

"Yep, I should."

"We're about to eat some pie."

"I could go for that," Henry said, bobbing his head. When he brushed past Lenny, he whispered, "Wanda was smiling to beat the band when she peeled into town. Just how bad is the new hairdo-over, anyway?"

"Pretty bad," Lenny said. "But don't let on. She's kinda sensitive about it."

Henry rounded the doorway to the kitchen then let out a cackle. "Did someone let a member of KISS off at the front door?"

"Very funny, Henry," Jane retorted. "Sit down and eat your pie."

Lenny had to smile. The life coach just might fit right in, after all.

TWO DAYS LATER, Jane sat on the bed in her room, thrilled that Lenny had given her the all clear to stay, not so thrilled that Lenny had also given her a racing heart and a thoroughly hot kiss.

And there was still the matter of that tell-all article for *Sidelined* magazine. Lenny had made it clear he didn't like media attention. An exposé on his life here would sure bring all kinds of attention. He'd never forgive her for betraying his trust, even if she didn't betray patient/client confidentiality.

Her guilt nagging at her like a burr in a bonnet, Jane looked over her notes. She didn't have to do the story. She'd told Bryan she wasn't so sure about this.

"We had an agreement," he reminded her.

"I never signed a contract," she retorted.

"I could ruin your reputation, Jane."

But Jane had held steady, insisting she was still working on getting Lenny to cooperate. And at this point, she wasn't so worried about her reputation as she was about Lenny's well-being. Was it worth risking her career to save a washed up football player?

She had to be the one to answer that particular question.

In spite of the imprinted memory of Lenny's lips on hers, she went back to her notes, her fingers gleefully typing away about the last two days of exercise, meals and spurts of cleaning clutter, with a few hints of Lenny's internal pain scattered here and there. Telling herself these notes were for her eyes only, Jane kept at it.

We had a breakthrough this week. I fell in the pond, but that won me some sympathy. That and

getting a makeover from Wanda Lawhorn. Memo
to self—Don't do that again, ever.

Jane stopped her work long enough to glance at herself in the tiny mirror by the bed. "Ugh." She'd brushed
the tangles and tease out of her hair over two days ago,
and now it fell in soft layers all around her face and
shoulders. "Not bad, if you don't notice the burgundy
highlights." Maybe a couple more washes would soften
that, too.

She went back to her work, typing from her hand-
written notes.

Mr. Paxton seems more willing to cooperate now.
Our fitness routine and new diet have brought a
healthy shine to his face, and we've managed to
pick through some of the clutter. Note to self—no
more sweet potato pie. Too many calories, even if
it does have fiber.

But, she thought, stopping to look out the window
at the golden autumn afternoon, the sweet potato pie
sure was good. Wondering exactly how close Ex-Wife
Number Two Barbara was to Lenny, Jane made a note
of that, too.

"Why do women cling to Lenny Paxton? Why does
this ex live on the premises? Hmm."

Hmm was right. Jane thought about the way he'd sat
there beside her on the stairs the other day, his long legs

clad in jeans, his easy country-boy drawl sending little notes of delight up and down her spine.

"Stop that," she told herself, rolling over on the bed to stare up at the ceiling fan. "Professional, Jane. You are a professional. And you've made some headway. Stick to the subject matter."

She *was* sticking to the subject matter. Because Lenny's image was front and center in her mind. If she could get past all of his defenses, they might get to the bottom of his problems about holding down marriages and keeping endorsement contracts and the whole hoarding issue.

> So with women, he's the love 'em and leave 'em type, but he stays close to a lot of women. And with agents and advertising executives, he's the fight 'em and make 'em angry type. But with his grandmother's personal things and all the things he'd managed to accumulate over his career, including women who love him, he's holding on for dear life.

"What's going on with you, Lenny?" she wondered, thinking she'd seen a side of him that most probably never saw. Except when she'd spoken about Bertie. He sure didn't want anyone messing with—

Jane came up off the bed. "With the woman who raised him!"

Lenny had admitted his grandparents had raised him.

Why? Where had his parents been? Come to think of it, she'd never found anything on his mother or father. Nothing in all the stories she'd found on him in both print and on the Internet. And the one time she'd questioned him about his mother, Lenny had gone ballistic. She needed to work on finding out about his parents.

A loud knock on her door startled Jane. Feeling both guilty and glad for what she'd figured out, she rushed to find Lenny standing there. "Hi," she said, hoping her expression didn't give away her curiosity.

"Hi." He rubbed a hand down the front of his flannel shirt, his gaze taking in her spiral notebook and the open laptop on the bed. "Listen, Barbara is here—"

Jane tried to hide her interest. "Oh, of course. Go on and do whatever…whatever it is you do with…uh…your second ex-wife. I'll be fine."

His smile was crooked. "Uh, what I mean…what I'm trying to say is…Barbara stops by now and then—to bring food mostly. She's here now, and well, she's dying to meet you. I'm going to check on the garden and some of the livestock—"

"You have livestock? I mean, besides hogs?"

"Uh, yes. Some horses and a few head of cattle."

"Oh, and your ex-wife wants to meet me?"

He shifted, looking back over his shoulder. "Yeah. She wants to see what a life coach looks like."

"Oh, well." She brushed at her hair. "Not so good right now, but that's nice, I think."

"You don't have to hang around with her. You can go with me."

Jane glanced around, then back to him. He looked so pained, she wondered if he had indigestion. "Oh, you're asking me to go for a walk with you?"

"I'm telling you that I'm going and if you want to come along then, yes, you're welcome to come—after you appease Barbara by saying hi."

Wow, did he have a way with words. Wondering how he managed to charm women when he always seemed so abrupt with her, she lifted her eyebrows. "And Barbara won't mind that?"

"Why should she? It's not like I'm taking you to Little Rock for a hot weekend."

"Of course, you're not." She grabbed her tiny notebook while she put images of being alone with him in Little Rock out of her mind. Seeing his frown aimed at her notebook, she said, "Only for notes. Nothing too personal. Just for observation."

He backed up, waving a hand toward the stairs. "Couldn't we just talk?"

She rushed out, closing the bedroom door with a bang. "Talking is good. We could do that, yes."

"I'm not a big talker," he said as they headed down the stairs.

A voice from the kitchen said, "You can sure say that again. Never could get him to talk to me very much when we were married."

Jane looked around the doorway to find an attractive,

petite blonde standing there with a cute, white-ruffled apron tied around her waist.

"Hi, I'm Barbara Paxton. Ex-wife number two."

"Oh, hello," Jane said, trying to hide her embarrassment. "It's nice to meet you. Your pie was wonderful."

Barbara's smile was pure sweetness. "Thank you. I do a pretty good business."

"Really?"

At Jane's confused look, Lenny said, "Barbara is a caterer. She sells pies all over Arkansas."

"Barbara's Baked Goods," Barbara answered, looking sheepish.

"You're Barbara's Baked Goods?" Jane asked, flabbergasted. "My mother is always buying your pies. She was thrilled when a local specialty store back home started carrying them."

Barbara giggled like a cheerleader. "I just started shipping on a regular basis. I'm branching out this year. Where's your mama from?" Her soft southern drawl was a pure delight.

"My whole family is from Arkansas," Jane said, reaching out to shake Barbara's hand. Which was decorated with one huge diamond solitaire.

"Oh, yes. I'm doing pretty good all over Arkansas and down in Louisiana. I have a whole new workspace for baking out behind the house—all the proper permits and equipment. My CPA is predicting a right nice increase in sales this year."

"You're a legend," Jane said, gushing. "Your baked goods are the 'it' thing within my mother's social circle."

"Well, thank you so much."

Lenny cleared his throat. "Uh, ladies, the sun's moving through the sky."

"Oh, never mind him," Barbara said. "Go on for your walk and take your time. I brought beef stew for dinner."

"I love beef stew," Jane replied, thrilled to meet the famous Barbara behind Barbara's Baked Goods. And such a modest, nice woman. And not exactly Lenny's type.

After chatting a few more minutes with Barbara, Jane still didn't get how someone like Lenny had married such a sweet woman like Barbara. And divorced her, too. More like Barbara had left him, probably.

"How'd you ever let her get away?" she asked Lenny the minute they hit the porch.

"Stupidity," he answered. "But, in case you haven't noticed, she didn't exactly get away. She lives right around the corner in a cute, tidy little farmhouse that we built together, but she remodeled and redecorated herself. A regular Southern-style Martha Stewart, that one. You two should hit it off just fine."

Jane planned on comparing notes. Lots of notes. But right now she had a question for Lenny. "So how do you do it?"

He pushed at a low pine branch. "Do what?"

"Keep women hanging on?"

He inched toward her, his grin full of mystery and triumph and that certain something that probably drew women to him. Jane could feel the pull when he leaned close and said in a slow-moving drawl, "Oh, now, Coach, if you stick around long enough, you just might get a chance to figure that out—whenever it's my turn to do some observing and note-taking. But I won't need this."

Then he took her notepad and tossed it in the rose-bush next to the back door.

CHAPTER SEVEN

"THIS IS YOUR FALL GARDEN?"

Jane looked at the weed-infested, crooked rows of what should have been newborn pumpkins, plump squash and freshly minted turnips and mustard greens. Instead it looked like an overgrown cluster of rogue shrubs. Boy had been shadowing them, and he unceremoniously relieved himself up against a tomato stake.

Lenny looked sheepish, his gaze down on his feet. "Yep. I can't farm."

"Then why are you trying?"

He shrugged, grabbed at some colorful ragweed. "I needed something to do, and I thought we could use the food."

The ragweed let loose a cluster of yellow blooms, causing Jane to hold her nose then let out a dainty sneeze. "Allergies," she said when Lenny shot her a puzzled look. "I thought Henry was helping you."

"He does help me with other things, like the cattle and the hogs. But he doesn't know about this."

Another interesting tidbit. "You have a secret garden?"

He rolled his shoulders then bent to tackle a stubborn

thistle bush. "Yes, I guess I do. And it's as disorganized as that old house back there."

An admission. That was good even if he did sound so defeated.

Boy spotted something in the nearby woods and took off running with a woof.

Jane watched the big awkward dog traipsing away, her heart hurting for Lenny. He was in more trouble than she thought if he'd stooped to sneaking in a fall garden. "Are you so short on funds that you have to resort to growing pumpkins?"

Shaking his head, he said, "Money, I got, sweetheart. I just wanted to stay busy. Something *with* my hands. Something away from everything. My grandfather Albert always had a garden, spring and fall."

"So you're trying to live up to his standards?"

"Is that a coach-type question, or do you really care?"

"Both," she said, trying to be honest. But she made a mental note, since he'd tossed her notebook. Luckily for her, she had a good memory for such details.

Lenny wanted to stay busy, yet he hadn't bothered to clean the house. Jane figured he escaped out to his garden in much the same way he escaped out to the pond to fish. And he played that annoying rock-and-roll music to drown out everything else. Lenny was running from everything and everyone. She had a clear picture of the situation. He'd built up clutter around the things from his childhood.

Jane imagined if she got past the old newspapers and magazines and the cabinets and storage bins, she'd find the drawers in the kitchen and the insides of the antique armoires neat and tidy—just the way Bertie had probably left them before she became so sick.

Lenny pushed at the wilted pumpkin vines. "My grandfather was the best farmer around these parts. He always had something going—chickens, pigs, cattle, hay fields and anything else that would grow in the ground. Plenty of corn and tomatoes, watermelons, all sorts of vegetables. When Bertie wasn't teaching, she was usually busy canning and freezing, or taking vegetables to the local farmer's market. That's how I grew up. That's the way it was until she got too sick to do any of that."

Another mental note. *That was how I grew up.* It was more the *way* he'd said that than the words that caught Jane's attention. "They made a good living here?"

He tossed a cracked tree limb out of the garden. "They held on, I reckon. And they always had me."

Jane noticed something that had been obvious all along, making another note in her head. This man would do anything to protect those he loved—and the place he loved. Maybe that was why his wives still hovered around him. But she wondered what price he would pay this time. He was doing the right thing, no doubt, by coming back here to lick his wounds. But watching someone he'd loved slowly deteriorate would surely have brought more complications to his already complicated life. Grief could really mess up a person. But his status had gone up a notch or two in Jane's mind because of the way he was trying to protect his grandparents' memory.

Stay professional, she warned herself. Wanting to broach the subject burning in her analytical mind, she asked, "What about your parents?"

Wrong question.

He started stomping toward the rows, yanking more thistle vines with a vengeance. "That topic is not open for discussion."

Jane could see him recoiling back into the cynical, uncaring man she'd met when she first arrived. So this must be the root of his issues. Wasn't that always the way? What had happened with his parents?

Deciding not to push him now, she grabbed at a patch of stubborn dandelions, her hands blistering from the effort, her eyes watering from the pollen and dust. But she kept on pulling, silent and sure, her breath steady as she followed him around.

Finally, he turned to glare at her, sweat popping out on his forehead, his thick hair curling against his skin. "Don't go all silent on me."

"I thought we were through talking."

He pointed a finger in the air. "You could drive a man crazy, doc."

She stood, stretching her back. "Oh? And how's that?"

He followed the line of the stretch—down and back up, his eyes going as soft as the autumn blue sky. "Oh, you know how. You and your busy mind, weaving stories and scenarios to figure people out. Well, you have no idea about me. You think I have issues with my parents. That's why you're suddenly so quiet. You're thinking too much. About me. And I don't want that."

"I've been weeding," Jane stated as she sniffed and dusted off her hands. "Nothing more. This is how we start, Lenny. One weed at a time. And right now, I'm trying to bring this garden back to life."

"Weeding, my foot. You're playing mind games, hoping I'll blurt it all out so you can understand me. But that ain't gonna happen."

"Could we talk about something else?" Jane asked with a firm smile. "Since this subject obviously upsets you."

He lifted his defiant chin. "You bet it does. And it's none of your business. I tried to tell you all along, I'm fine here."

She looked down at a wilted pumpkin vine. "Of course it's not any of my business, and of course, you're just fine. Anyone can see that."

He let out a distinct chuckle, brittle and echoing. "You can stop now."

"Stop what?"

"Stop trying to convince me that you don't care. You've got that patronizing, *analyze-this* tone in your voice."

She put her hands on her hips and enjoyed a bit of the breeze sweeping through the pines and cottonwood trees. "Why should I try to analyze anything about you? You've made it very clear I'm not to mention that subject again. But apparently that subject is the source of all of your angst. Let's just work on this garden."

He gave her a suspicious look, started to speak then clamped his mouth shut. Then he started pulling weeds again.

While Jane stayed quiet and tossed the dandelions and buttercups she'd gathered off into the brush.

HE SHOULD HAVE KNOWN she wasn't through with him.

Lenny found the note early the next morning.

It said, in her crisp, concise handwriting, *Lenny, meet me at the garden. Bring your hoe.* Signed, *Jane.*

The garden. She'd said time and time again they needed to go through the house and clean it before the health department came out here to condemn it. Not that he lived in filth. Bertie had taught him better than that. No, he just worked around the clutter. The clutter brought him comfort, but he wasn't about to admit that. The clutter felt like being back in the huddle ten yards from the end zone, itching for a score.

But having a woman around day and night, well, that made him feel exposed and definitely defenseless and itching for another kind of score. No teammates, no coach here. Except the little life coach, of course. She wanted to tear down all his defenses. And she wanted to know the story about his parents. That was a story he wasn't ready to tell. Not even to her. He refused to discuss that. He would not think about the sordid tale of his parents. Or lack of parents.

Lenny didn't know much about farming, but he sure knew women. They were always making some sort of play. Just when you thought you had women figured out, they'd fake you out and wait for you to go deep. Too deep.

He'd been scoring with women most of his life. And running from them, too. Maybe that was his biggest problem.

Henry ambled into the kitchen just as Lenny tossed the note in the trash. "You ain't gone yet?"

"I haven't decided *if* I'm going."

"Well, I'm here now," Henry said, pouring some coffee. "I know the routine. If a stranger shows up, shoot first and ask questions later."

"Especially if it's an agent or a sportswriter," Lenny said, nodding. "Then you can help me bury the bodies, too."

"I've got a shovel in the truck," Henry replied with a grin.

Glancing around, Lenny asked, "Have you seen Boy?"

"He headed off with the life coach. I think she's trying to give him lessons in obedience."

"Same here," Lenny quipped, his tone grim.

"I'd say she's got a better chance with the dog."

"I hear that." Lenny glanced around, grabbed an

apple, then started for the door. But he pivoted to stare at Henry. "How'd you know to come this morning?"

Henry glanced up. "That life coach. She called me late yesterday with a schedule."

His hand on the door, Lenny turned. "Excuse me? What kind of schedule?"

"Said y'all were going to get the garden into shape—I didn't even know you had a garden—and get on with clearing out the house. Then she said something about painting and rearranging the kitchen. I think she wanted me here to referee or something."

Lenny felt the hair stand up on the back of his neck. Controlling, was his little life coach. He didn't do controlling, not with women, anyway. "What else did the good doctor say?"

"Not much. She's a bright ball of fire, that one. She was moving the whole time she was talking. Hard to pin her down."

"Yep," Lenny said, anger warring with admiration in his mind. Maybe it was time for one of *his* lessons. 'Cause he figured the only way he'd get this infuriating woman out of his mind was to just have at it, give her his all—technique-wise. Lenny Paxton was famous for his moves, after all. Both on the football field and off.

He left, stalking down toward the garden across from the pond, wondering what she had cooked up this time. Gardening he could handle, even if he couldn't grow spit.

But he wasn't so sure about all the other stuff she

kept mentioning. And he was really mad that his own sorry excuse of a loyal companion, Boy, had deserted him to tag along with the cute little coach.

He found her with a hoe in her hand, working away at what was left of his pumpkins and squash. But he had to admit, the turnips and mustard greens looked halfway lively this morning.

"A little rain would help," she said by way of a greeting.

Boy barked in agreement, close at her heels while Lenny admired her backside.

"We'll get some soon. Always comes around October. Sometimes, we get bad storms." Like the one standing in his garden.

She reached for the huge watering bucket Lenny kept on the back porch. "I don't need a storm. Just some moisture for these dehydrated vegetables."

He watched as she wet the ground around the vegetables, thinking she'd do better to drag a hose down here. "So you know how to farm, too?"

She finally lifted up to stare at him, leaning onto her hoe handle. Her hair was a mess, all windblown and tousled and a little curly from the morning dew. She wasn't wearing any makeup, but the crisp autumn air had her cheeks a rosy red. She wore another tight little urban-designed workout suit that fit her nice and snug, with a zipped black jacket to match.

Lenny prayed she'd keep the jacket on, but from the way sweat was beading on her pretty upper lip, he had a feeling she'd be removing layers any minute now. And he didn't want to have to admire her sweet curves.

"How long you been at this?" he asked, stooping to pick up the colorful array of discarded weeds she'd managed to conquer. Noting she'd brought along a black trash bag to gather the trimmings, he could at least admire her thoroughness.

"I got out here around six. I'm an earlier riser."

"Humph." He didn't doubt that. Probably never let loose with a night on the town, this one. She was all about schedules and purpose. Nothing wasted. It figured that shrinks never slept anyway. Too busy making charts and notes and picking away at people's defenses. Too busy trying to figure out ways to torture him into cracking like an egg.

Giving his guilty-looking dog the evil eye, he said, "You should have cleared this with me." And he was talking to *both* of them.

She stopped hoeing, probably because he'd said that with an angry tone. "Weeding? This is *my* therapy. I used to love to do yard work at my parents' house. It gives me time and solitude, helps me to think."

"I'm not talking about weeds or yard work."

Jane leaned both hands on the handle of her hoe. "Then what are you talking about?"

Boy's big ears perked up as if the dog knew this was getting better by the minute.

"This schedule stuff," Lenny said, reaching out a hand to Boy. "I never agreed to any kind of schedule."

"So you're angry that I took matters into my own hands? I told you—this week, exercise and diet, and next week, everything organized. And that means getting into a disciplined routine. We have to start from the inside out so we can get to the root of the real problems."

"I don't like surprises. Henry was a surprise."

"I only asked Henry to come and do his 'bouncer' thing while you and I took care of this and got in our morning workout. Although for the life of me, I don't understand why Henry just shows up at your house each morning. Or why his being here this morning could be called a surprise."

Lenny wasn't about to explain that to her. He gritted his teeth so tight, he could feel his pulse pounding inside his temple. "I don't recall agreeing to going through Bertie's things. And besides, when are we going to get back to my part of this little project?" Taking a breath, he moved toward her, reaching out an inviting hand. "I say let's knock off and go have a big breakfast. Barbara loves to cook me breakfast."

She looked appalled. "I will not bother Barbara this morning. You need to learn how to cook for yourself. And since when does a grown man have to have bouncers and watchers and pampering ex-wives all around? It's not like you're Brad Pitt, you know."

Lenny wondered how he ever thought she looked attractive. This woman had him by the throat and she obviously didn't intend to let go. What could he do? Kidnap her and hide her in the barn? Take her to the county line and leave her? Take her snipe hunting? Since he couldn't make her go away, Lenny was determined to make her pay. Oh, yeah, soon the tables were gonna turn.

"You've gotten soft, Lenny. If you intend to get that spokesperson contract firmed up—"

"I don't intend to do any such thing," he shouted, tossing weeds in the air. Boy took off to catch whatever was being tossed, then turned back, looking confused. "I'm letting you do your organization thing. But you weren't supposed to bring up all that other stuff." Then he took the hoe from her and started chopping away. "I intend to get out of that contract. I don't want to be tied down with a long-term commitment that would require traveling."

"It would mean a lot of money."

"I told you, I got money."

"But don't you want to show the world—"

He grabbed her hand in midair, causing her to drop the bundle of crabgrass she'd unearthed. "Stop right there. You have no idea what you're talking about. Why do I need to show the world anything? Why can't I just live my life, right here?"

She didn't flinch, and she didn't back down. Instead she kept looking directly into his eyes, her gaze even and level. "You can do that, but with a healthy attitude. Has it ever occurred to you that Marcus was truly concerned about you when he called me?"

He clutched her hand, his nostrils flaring. "Oh, right.

You think my attitude isn't healthy. You and Marcus and the entire world can't seem to grasp that a man just needs to rest." He eased toward her then, going gentle enough to throw her off. "I have a good attitude, doc. Very good. And when we've finished this garden work, it's my turn to show you a thing or two."

He was rewarded when she swallowed and went silent, her eyes going wide and changing colors like a falling leaf. "That might take a long time."

He gave her the same level gaze back. "Then that's how long we'll be here."

"Okay, then." He hated the edge of fear he saw in her eyes. "You still think if you flirt with me and ply me with pretty words, I'll bolt. But I'm tougher than that."

"Oh, yeah?" he said, tugging her close. He stared down at her long enough to enjoy her rose-petal blush. "Well, we'll see, won't we? Today, we hoe and clean. Tonight, after the game, we dance and swing. Deal?"

He wondered what she was thinking, but he didn't dare ask. Instead, he returned to nurturing the garden. Being able to take out his frustrations on weeds and dirt seemed to help alleviate some of his anxieties. So he kept at it, pushing all his worries out of his mind as the autumn sunshine pushed through the sky in a halo of shimmering gold.

Then he felt Jane's hand on his arm. "Lenny, you can stop now."

He looked up to find himself at the end of the last

row. The garden was clean and sparkling fresh. Jane had gone behind him watering and he hadn't even realized it.

"I'll go draw more water from the pond," she said, her gaze moving over the neat rows. "And then we'll call it a day with the garden work. And after that—"

She didn't get to finish. His phone rang, causing him to hold up a hand to silence her.

"Yeah?"

"It's Henry. Get back here quick. We got unexpected company. And I can't shoot this one."

"I'm on my way." Lenny closed the phone and shouted over his shoulder. "I've got to go back to the house."

Lenny didn't wait around for her to follow. Instead he stomped the short distance to the house, his heart jarring like a band at halftime. His knees began to protest but he kept on going. And he could hear Jane moving right behind him, with Boy barking behind her.

Taking the back steps two at a time, he skidded into the kitchen.

And found Henry cleaning up dishes at the sink. His first ex-wife was standing there dressed to the nines in clothes his money had paid for, staring at Henry with her defiant big green eyes.

Now, at least, he understood why Henry had called him. His grandmother had never approved of Candace Kelly and neither did his friend Henry. Neither did his two other ex-wives, although they tolerated her visits. Come to think of it, nobody he knew liked Candace. So

what had been the big attraction for him? Oh, yeah—
there was that knockout figure. Big mistake, this one.
Even bigger mistake that she'd showed up at his door
and with the life coach here, too. Big mistake.

"Candace?" he began.

Then the back door slammed and in walked Jane
Harper, her analytical little brain making her autumn
eyes grow wide with interest. "Hello."

Boy came rushing in with Jane, took one look at
the exotic woman tapping her heels against the kitchen
linoleum and growled. Very loudly.

Boy had never approved of Candace, either.

CHAPTER EIGHT

JANE TOOK IN THE SCENE.

Henry, looking scared and apologetic, cleaning the dishes with a mighty scouring. Lenny appeared drained and damaged, as if this was not what he wanted today. Boy, sniffing and growling near Lenny's feet.

And that woman.

Jane could only describe the woman standing there as a cross between someone out of the *Dynasty* cast and a show-girl she'd once seen at a party back in Little Rock.

Henry glanced around, his expression pinched. "I tried to tell her no. She came on in anyway. Then she got all bent out of shape when I told her you weren't here."

"I'm not all bent out of shape," the woman said, waving red-lacquered fingertips. "I just happened to be in the neighborhood—"

Boy turned and growled again then advanced a step, his teeth bared.

The woman actually looked scared. "Lenny, call off that impossible dog, okay? C'mon, honey. It's just me."

Jane wasn't sure if the woman was speaking to the

dog or the man, since they both had the same threatening grimace on their faces.

Henry tossed a paper towel in the trash. "I guess I'll be going now. Sorry, Lenny."

"What in the world is he doing here, anyway?" the woman asked. "I thought after Bertie passed—"

"That's enough," Lenny said, pointing a finger toward the woman. "Not another word about Bertie."

The woman shut up, but put a hand on her hip as her gaze moved over the room. "Man, everyone sure is touchy around here, and when was the last time you cleaned this place, anyway?" Then she zoomed in on Jane. "Interesting hairdo. I guess you've had one of Wanda's famous makeovers, too."

Jane didn't want to discuss that. "Thanks, Henry," she said, ushering him to the door. The woman gave her a look that was both dismissive and curious then focused her attention back on Lenny.

Henry leaned close and whispered. "Watch it, Coach. That one is bad news."

Jane nodded. "I'll keep that in mind."

She turned around to Lenny, fascinated by the way he and the woman seemed to be at a standoff.

"Lenny?" There was a long whine in his name as the woman threw her bronzed metallic leather bag onto the table. "What's going on?"

"What are you doing here, Candace?" Lenny asked, moving away. Not waiting for an answer, he held the advancing woman at arm's length. "You know I don't like surprise visits."

Candace gave him a long pout. "I told you, suga', I was just passing through. It's been such a long time."

Petulance personified, Jane noted. And such a stereotypical spoiled rich girl, it wasn't even challenging. An easy mark for a womanizer like Lenny. Or maybe Lenny had been the easy mark in this case. From the look in the woman's eyes, she still had it bad for the football player.

"I've told you, don't come here without calling first. This place isn't exactly on the beaten path. You went way out of your way. And I want to know why."

Jane cleared her throat. "Maybe I should leave you two alone?"

Lenny looked up first. "No, you stay right here, Coach."

"If you say so," Jane said, smiling softly to waylay the killer glare she was getting from Candace. Something about Lenny's command for her to stay gave Jane the strength to meet that withering look head-on. Strictly for research purposes, of course.

"Coach? *This* is the life coach?" Candace sank down on a chair then crossed her long legs, her burgundy patent leather stilettos shimmering and winking.

The woman had legs for days. Candace was as gussied up as Wanda Lawhorn had been, but where Wanda's clothes had been gaudy and harsh, this woman's outfit spoke of lots of money. She was clad from head to toe in designer threads, from her tight green cashmere sweater to her beige pencil skirt. And the whole package was wrapped in shimmering gold jewelry and a swatch of long, brilliant red hair that almost matched her shoes.

"I'm sorry, I don't think we've been formally introduced," Jane said, extending her hand. "I'm Jane Harper."

"Oh, my." Candace took Jane's hand for a brief shake while her gaze trailed over Jane with a steamroller force. "I'm Candace Kelly Paxton, the *first* ex-wife."

Jane let that information roll over her right along with the appraising look, but she managed to maintain a straight face. "Nice to meet you."

Candace tossed her hair. "Whatever." Then she slid her gaze back to Lenny. "It's just that you've been stuck here—" She stopped, lifting model-perfect eyebrows toward Jane. "Do you mind?"

Jane took the hint and this time she wouldn't let Lenny keep her here. "No, not at all. But, Lenny, we still have work to do."

Giving him her full attention by turning away from Candace, she said, "I'd like to go over some of my suggestions regarding our activity routine, but we can do that…after you're finished here." She shot Candace what she hoped was a dismissive look.

Candace let out a snort. "Activity routine? Is that what a life coach calls it? Y'all sure have a strange way of talking about—"

"It's not what you think," Lenny said, a tad too

defensive for Jane's taste. "Jane is here to help me sort through some things."

"Isn't that special," Candace said, swinging her foot as she reclined like a cat back in her chair. Then she sent Lenny a glamorous smile. "Suga', I used to be good at helping you sort through things. How 'bout I help out some now?"

Jane rolled her eyes then gave Lenny a calculated stare. "I'll be up in my room, *making notes.*"

Before he could protest again, she whirled to head up the stairs. After all, it didn't take a highly trained professional to figure out that ex-wife number one was still hot for Lenny, but how did he feel about Candace? Jane didn't have to stay around for the rest of the conversation, no matter how much Lenny wanted her there as a buffer. The man sure liked buffers.

"Notes on what?" Candace said, loud enough of course, for Jane to hear. "How boring is that!"

Jane thought about giving Candace a few verbal pointers, but she didn't. Easing the door to her room shut, she had to wonder which ex-wife would pop up next.

"Not your problem," Jane said, plopping on her bed to open her laptop while she tried to put the memory of Lenny kissing her out of her mind. But then the image of him being with Candace took its place. "Just make your notes." *Note to self—don't let nasty ex-wife comments undermine your intent here. Stick to the plan.* And don't compare yourself to that creature sitting downstairs.

Jane decided to make a list. If she did write an article for *Sidelined,* what would she include in it?

First, Lenny needed professional guidance on how best to deal with his obvious obsessive-compulsive issues.

Second, Lenny needed emotional support and encouragement as he worked through the internal problems that had brought him to this point. She could continue to give him suggestions on how to deal with all the stress and emotional burdens that has caused his initial meltdown.

Third, Lenny obviously had long-held issues regarding his parentage and women. Jane could talk him through those and help him get to the root of why he couldn't commit to a lasting, meaningful relationship. This would be of major importance if he wanted to truly heal.

Fourth, make sure this thousand-watt attraction she felt for the man did not manifest into something she wouldn't be able to control.

And fifth, figure out the ex-wife angles. That should keep her mind off the man who'd married all of them. Then maybe the ex-wives could be dealt with accordingly and Lenny would find the courage to go back out into the world.

Okay, he wasn't exactly hiding. He was trying to protect the last shreds of his life. That brought Jane straight out of her professional mode and right into dangerous territory. His sacrifice was impressive and noble, which meant he did have some redeeming qualities. She'd be the one in denial if she didn't stop to acknowledge that. As a woman. As a counselor. As both. *Sigh*.

Lenny Paxton was hiding away to protect his own vulnerabilities and the memories he held so dear. Apparently, his grandmother's illness and death had triggered some long-held emotions that had caused him to back out of the endorsement contract. He wasn't shirking his duties; he wasn't giving up the limelight because he believed himself to be a has-been. He was doing the right thing for himself, or at least he thought.

How could she expose all that by writing an in-depth article about him in a national sports magazine? And why did she ever agree to such a thing in the first place?

But, she thought, she could write about her experiences here in general terms. How she helped him get his grandparents' estate back in shape. How she helped him deal with a near meltdown from overexposure and too many relationship problems? Would he go for that at least?

She would have to research Lenny's past some more. Dig a little deeper. Lenny was hiding something so personal that he'd somehow managed to keep it out of the press.

And Jane would keep it out of the press, too.

But she needed to know what that something was, so she could help him. So she could see him smile. Lenny had a good, strong smile, magazine cover quality. But he only half used it these days.

Feeling better for tightening her plan of action, Jane decided to take a quick bath and get on with her day. First thing, she'd call Bryan Culver and tell him the magazine deal was off for now.

LENNY COULDN'T TAKE HIS EYES off the woman sitting with cougarlike alertness across from him. Candace was a beauty, no doubt. But then she had been born and bred in Texas, with her daddy's oil money to burn and a bought-and-paid-for charm school persona that could turn roadhouse-mean in a heartbeat. She was still his favorite mistake.

And he had to get rid of her immediately, or he'd be making another mistake. "Candace, you can't do this."

"Do what, darlin'? I just wanted to see you. You don't call, you don't write. I was missing you."

"Candy," he said, hoping using that pet name would soften things, "I told you last time we talked that I wouldn't be traveling anymore for a while. That I would be out of touch."

She pouted and primped, applying more luscious lipstick to her already moist lips. "You didn't say it would be forever. I swear I thought you'd forgotten me altogether." Then she sent him a look that told him that would be nearly impossible.

Which was true.

Candace was both a blessing and a curse. He'd married her right after he'd signed his first big-league contract. They'd both had money to burn, and being young and full of life and lust, they'd made a striking couple. But it had all burned out in the first couple of years.

Too much of a good thing could be hard on a man. And Candace was way too much of a good thing. She still had Daddy's money along with a lot of Lenny's now, too.

"You can't stay," he said, holding his hands together over his knees.

She winked and grinned. "Why? You already got a houseful?"

He didn't miss the way she glanced toward the stairs.

"Why are you here, Candace?"

She leaned forward, her painted lips pretty and inviting. "Honestly, suga', I was worried about you. Marcus seems to think—"

"Don't tell me Marcus called you?"

"No, I called him looking for you. He was worried, too. When he told me about this silly life coach thing, I had to come see for myself."

Lenny saw trouble all the way around. No wonder Boy had taken off for the back of the house. Cowardly dog. But Lenny couldn't blame the mutt. He wanted to run, too. He always wanted to run. Only, this time he couldn't do that. He was shocked to discover that he was willing to fight for Jane.

"You can't stay," he told Candace again. "And don't tell me you just dropped by. I know you travel with at least three suitcases anyway."

She laughed, tipped her head. "Well, you never know where I might lay my head."

He got up, gripped the back of the chair. "Oh, I know, baby. I remember very well where you laid your head when we were together. That's why I divorced you."

"You're being such an old grouch about this," Candace said, jumping up to slink toward him. "Just send the life coach away, and we can start all over again."

Lenny laughed out loud. He couldn't stop laughing. He laughed so loud, he was afraid he'd bring Jane running down the stairs. Then he stopped laughing, remembering it was hard to smile these days, let alone laugh. He'd tried to send the life coach away, hadn't he?

"You need to leave," he told Candace, grabbing her oversized, overpriced purse as he dragged her by the arm toward the door. "Just get into that sweet little Mercedes and go on back across the state line to Texas, sweetheart."

She dug in her stilettos. "I…I don't want to leave."

"Oh, but you are, whether you want to or not. You came here to pick on my life coach, didn't you? You're jealous. Not a very pretty quality."

"I am so not jealous," Candace said, her gaze moving from him straight up the stairs as a door opened. "Why would I be jealous of *that?*"

Lenny turned to find Jane standing at the top of the

stairs, wearing yet another set of clingy sweatpants and matching tight knit top, a clipboard in one hand and her BlackBerry in the other. Her hair was rustled and scattered, reminding him of leaves in a November wind. She wore black-framed reading glasses and jotted notes like there was no tomorrow. Where did she get another notebook, anyway? And why did her glasses make her even more sexy?

"What's she doing?" Candace said, her suspicious words whispering across Lenny's edgy nerve endings.

He snickered again. It struck him as funny, that adorable way Jane had of looking so serious and determined in the midst of chaos and confusion. At least he knew where he stood with her. That was kind of refreshing.

Before he could answer, however, things went into overtime.

"Me?" Jane asked, practically skipping down the stairs. "I'm doing my job."

"And what exactly is that job?" Candace asked right back. "I mean, why in the world would Lenny need a life coach?" She centered her sultry gaze on him. "He's in pretty good shape as far as I can tell."

Lenny watched Jane while Candace let her gaze slip and slide down his body. Jane seemed fascinated, as if she were studying monkeys in the zoo. And Lenny supposed they did kind of look and act like that.

"He's in very good shape," Jane replied, so serious. But she also let her gaze slide over his entire body. And now he did feel as if he were on display. Two very different women eying him with delicious intent. It almost did him in. But he enjoyed winking at only one.

Jane.

He should have said something, done something. But lately, there had been too many women coming and going around here and he was fast losing his grip on reality. He wasn't as quick on his feet as he used to be. Maybe he was having his nineteenth nervous breakdown, after all.

Too late, he saw that little spark of challenge in Jane's eyes as she pivoted, prim and proper, toward Candace. "My job here is simple. I'm helping Lenny get to the root of all of his issues. I'm going to decipher his psyche to find out why, for starters, he can't seem to stay married. I'm trying to teach him some behavior modification so that he can handle stress much better than he has in recent situations and I've put him on a light exercise program to improve upon his already healthy physical attributes. And somewhere in there, we're going to continue cleaning this house and get all this clutter in place so he can have a fresh start in a calm nurturing environment."

Snapping her pen shut, she lifted her head to give Candace a brilliant smile that beamed right through her bi-focals. "In other words, I'm going to get rid of the dead weight." She said this with emphasis on the *dead weight* while she purposely graced Candace with a dismissive glare. "Any more questions?"

Lenny had never seen Candace speechless before. Her mouth opened, but she didn't move. He thought she'd probably forgotten how to breathe. This was actually pretty entertaining stuff.

So he started laughing all over again. Not so loud this time. But a soft gentle chuckle that started deep inside his stomach and worked its way up to his throat.

He didn't even stop when he saw Candace's perfectly tanned skin turn two shades brighter than her hair.

"Are you laughing at me, Lenny?"

Lenny shook his head. "Nah, baby. I'm laughing at everything. And you have no idea how good it feels to laugh."

Then because she had done such a number on Candace, Lenny grabbed Jane and lifted her into the air, holding her up so high her Nikes didn't even touch the floor as he spun her around. Realizing what he was doing and how both Candace and Jane stared at him— one as if he'd lost his mind and the other with big luminous hazel-hued eyes full of longing and need—he placed Jane back down on the floor, sure that same need was sizzling back to her from his eyes.

He'd stopped laughing, his mind filling with other ideas.

Candace finally twitched into action, bringing her hands to her mouth as she came toward him with all the finesse of a skittish cat on the attack. "What on earth has this woman done to you, darlin'?"

From the look of utter shock on her face, Jane was

about as flustered as Candace. But she quickly regained her footing. Fluffing her hair back with her hand, she slanted her head to one side. "I think we've just had a breakthrough. You laughed, Lenny. You *were* laughing. I haven't witnessed what could be termed a real laugh from you since I've been here. That's a very good sign and so important for relieving tension."

Lenny laughed again, because she had no idea, no idea at all what she was doing to him. He knew all about relieving tension. He'd been married three times, hadn't he? And if he could just have his way with her—

Candace wasn't laughing, however, not one bit. "I'm not leaving now, that's for sure."

"Yes, you are," Lenny said, still grinning. "I don't have room for any ex-wives."

"But you have room for her?"

"Yes, I do. She's the life coach. We had a breakthrough."

Candace tipped toward him, her stilettos hitting against the hardwood floor. "But you were laughing before she came downstairs, remember? So technically that means I helped you with your breakthrough."

"It doesn't work that way," Lenny said, backing her toward the door. He gave her a soft peck on the forehead. "Goodbye, Candy."

"You can't just throw me out."

"Yes, I can. I've got enough trouble without you hanging around here."

Candace gave Jane a look that could have melted the bark off a pine tree. "This is your fault."

"I accept full responsibility," Jane replied, smug and sure. "And I can assure you, you're not needed here."

That only made Candace fume even more. "Lenny?"

"You can't stay in this house, Candy. You know the rules. Bertie never allowed such stuff when she was alive and I won't allow it now that we're not married. She might be gone, but she never allowed for hanky-panky under her roof."

Candace gave him a pretty pout. "Bertie hated me."

"She didn't hate you. She just didn't approve of you."

Candace tried another tactic. "Well, then why don't you remember the rules and kick this woman out, too. You're acting like an idiot and well, she's doing something to you, Lenny. She's got you all mixed up."

Lenny cut a gaze toward Jane. "Yep, she sure has, at that."

Candace's keen gaze moved from him to Jane and back, her cat eyes changing as if she'd seen something distasteful. Finally her slender shoulders sank in defeat—a rare sight, that. "This isn't over."

"I know, honey. It's never over with you."

"I'm going to find Barbara and get her take on this."

"Have at it."

"I bet she'll let me stay at her place."

"Probably so."

"Is it wise to let two of your ex-wives stay together?"

"Probably not, but they like to gang up on me."

"He doesn't care," Candace said, her voice a whining drawl. "He knows we'll just sit up all night eating chocolate and comparing notes on *him*." Then she gave an eloquent shrug. "Shoot, you might as well join us. That's definitely the best way to figure out Lenny Paxton. Just spend an afternoon with some of his ex-wives."

Lenny didn't like the conniving light shining in Candy's slanted eyes. She was up to something.

"What kind of chocolate?" Jane asked, oblivious to yet another trap. Or maybe not.

"Oh, I like dark and Barbara, well, she loves milk. Luckily, she keeps both on hand. She'll probably whip up a killer batch of brownies, too."

"Hmm. I like dark." Jane nodded, jotted notes. "Maybe I'll walk over sometime for tea."

Candace clutched her bag then pivoted with model-like precision, talking as she turned. "Right. Tea. You don't even have to call first. Just come on over."

"Okay, thanks," Jane said, her smile as sweet as molasses.

Sensing interference, Lenny said, "Uh, Candy, wait—"

Candace kept walking, prissy as a hen. "This isn't over, Lenny. I mean it. I'm going to Barbara's."

"Tell her I said hello," Lenny retorted, his chuckle weakening to a pasted grin as he called her bluff.

"I sure will." Candace gave them one last glance, then headed out the door, slamming it behind her.

"That went well," Jane said, tucking her pen in her hair. "I definitely have to get them together for a talk. It's obvious your ex-wives are enabling you to the point of overindulgence."

Lenny's burst of sheer joy ended and his world went as silent as an empty stadium.

CHAPTER NINE

"DO YOU WANT SOME LUNCH?"

Lenny turned to where Jane stood in the middle of the kitchen, looking as efficient as ever in spite of the bizarre, busy morning they'd had. Her hair had settled into a fluffy shag around her face and shoulders, the burgundy highlights softening with each wash.

He thought about how she'd felt in his arms earlier and about how much he wanted to kiss her again. Instead, Lenny gave her a tight smile then clicked his pen open and shut to the tune of Johnny Cash singing "I Walk the Line" on the radio. They were both walking the line today.

"I'm not hungry," he said. He'd just finished paying some bills and checking in with the hundred and ten people who wanted a piece of him. Jane had insisted he start small and work his way through some of the mail. And he had to admit it felt good, getting the stacks cleared away. It took his mind off other things, like her perfume and her hair and her lips. And all that he needed to tell her, but couldn't.

Slapping his laptop shut, he turned to face her. "Sorry about Candace."

She gave him a blank look. "You certainly don't have to apologize to me. She's *your* ex."

"Then maybe I should be telling myself I'm sorry."

She shook her head as she sat down, her infernal notebook close at hand. "Never mind Candace. I've made us a chart."

He let out a long sigh. "I told you I don't do charts anymore."

"I'm not talking about a play chart."

Pushing a hand through his hair, he leaned forward. No point in explaining a playbook to her. "We had a breakthrough, so why are you torturing me so much?"

She tapped her pen on the notebook. "We need a few more breakthroughs."

He lifted his eyebrows in a frown. "You caught me in a weak moment. That breakthrough earlier made me tired."

She sat back, crossing her arms. "Well, after what happened this morning, I don't doubt that."

"Oh, yeah. Candace is a pain, that's for sure."

"No, not Candace. She is not my concern. But you are."

He had to swallow at the soft way she'd said that. When was the last time anyone had been truly concerned about him? He knew the answer to that. It shouted at him each time he walked through this old, cluttered, creaking house. But he didn't want to talk about any of it.

"I'm doing all right, Coach." He held up a hand when

she opened her mouth to contradict that statement. "I can see now that I've been avoiding some things. But I can handle my ex-wives." He wanted to add that the only woman getting to him right now was the one staring across the table at him. He'd love to run his hands through that new hairdo of hers and give her something really good to write in that notebook.

"We need to learn how to avoid scenes like the one this morning," Jane said in her firm, no-nonsense coaching way. "You handled it pretty well, I have to admit. But going into hysterical laughter is not a good sign."

"I thought you were glad I laughed."

"I was. But I also saw the little bit of anger in your eyes when you were laughing. You don't like anyone bringing up people you've lost, Lenny. Especially Bertie."

"Bertie never did like Candace. And Bertie was a good judge of character. I didn't need Candace reminding me."

"I'm with you there." Then she leaned forward. "Want to talk about it?"

Not wanting to delve into his fatalist attraction to a woman nicknamed Candy, Lenny decided no, he didn't want to talk about it, so he changed the subject. "Show me the chart."

"Nice save," Jane said, grinning.

She really was pretty when she smiled. Or laughed. Or just sat there with her ink pen. Denying that, he said, "Let's get on with this." Then he tapped a finger on the table. "And remember, we have a date for dinner after the big game—my turn to…uh…coach you."

She looked dazed for a minute then perked up immediately, ignoring his flirtation. "Well, I've gone over everything regarding the organizational process. You've done a good job with the garden and now some of the mail. Time to finish up here in the kitchen. And hopefully, we can get to the heart of the matter—why you've been hoarding all of this stuff since Bertie died."

"I've already tried to explain that."

"No, you've been making excuses. Excuses won't get your life back in order."

He couldn't dispute that. And he was tired of fighting it. And her. "Okay. You're right. No more excuses. So what's next?"

Her soft, sure smile was his reward for the day. "Look around, Lenny. You have priceless antiques everywhere, not to mention football trophies and awards and all kinds of mementoes from your career. This place is a testament to both your life and Bertie and Albert's. Bertie's dolls should be displayed and protected." She put down her notebook. "It's really just a matter of taking one room at a time and finding a proper place for everything."

"Is that how it works?" he asked, honestly wanting to know. "If I do this, will my life miraculously fall into place? Or are you trying to find a compartment for Lenny Paxton, too?"

She leaned forward, her hair shining around her

face like gold-and-russet velvet. "No, I'm trying to *free* Lenny Paxton to live his life to the fullest."

"Well, I've never had a woman say that to me before," he retorted, loving that hair. Maybe Wanda had hit on something, spicing the life coach up like that. And just because he was in a teasing, coaching kind of mood himself, he leaned close. "I kind of like that, Coach. You know, you and me, we might have more in common than you thought, huh?"

He was rewarded with a flustered look and a definite lifting of her dark eyebrows. "What we have in common is getting you straight, Lenny."

"Good luck with that," he said. And as he said it, he reached out to push a sprig of hair away from her cheek. "You look nice today."

Jane lifted away, but her gaze held his, her sweet eyes as unsure as a doe caught in the woods. "Thanks."

Score a touchdown for the aged quarterback.

But she recovered nicely. "Okay, so the plan is to get the kitchen clean since that seems to be where everyone winds up. We'll take our time. No rush."

"None at all," he replied, enjoying this. "I like taking my time."

She gave him a look full of disbelief coupled with a bit of hope. "Is that how you wound up with three ex-wives? By taking your time?"

Okay, field goal for the little lady. He was behind and running out of time-outs. So he decided to be honest.

"No, I wound up with three ex-wives because I'm hard to live with and I'm not very good husband material."

She jotted something in her notebook. "I wouldn't have guessed—"

"Oh, and I reckon you have ideas on that, too."

"I do," she said, back to being studious and stern. "Quite a few."

Because he wanted to keep flirting with her, he lowered his voice. "Go ahead, show me some of your moves."

Jane tilted her head. "If you'll allow me to make a few observations—you seem to love the chase much more than the conquest. I think you can't make a commitment to just one woman because you're still searching for the perfect woman."

Lenny grinned big. "Is there such a creature?"

"No, and that's the point. You have to find a nice balance. Same with this house. You wanted it to stay perfect, the way it was when Bertie and Albert were alive, but when she died things were no longer perfect. So you gave up. You've managed to cover over what you thought was perfect with all this mess. But together, we can fix it."

Her words, spoken with such clarity and authority, hit Lenny like a blitzing linebacker. She'd summed things up, but she'd also told him how to fix things. With her help. That "we" in her words meant a lot to him.

"I was the same way playing the game. I wanted things to go perfect, but it didn't always turn out that way. I've managed to mess up my life pretty bad in the process."

He saw the triumph in her eyes, but he also saw something that tore at his gut even more. Compassion.

"Nothing that can't be resolved," she said, her words hushed. "People who seek perfection often give up when they can't figure out how to reach it. You walked out on an important deal but you've always lived up to your obligations—in your career at least. Right now you're transferring. You want things to be perfect and here I am trying to make you see that—me being a perfectionist myself—so you're taking out all of your frustration on me, and the garden and this house, too."

Ignoring the part about his sagging career and his need for perfection gone wrong and the fact that he was taking that out on her, he zoomed in on the obligation part. "But I haven't always lived up to my personal obligations, huh?"

She sat up, clasping her hands together. "Give the man a cigar. I think he's beginning to get it."

Lenny glared a tight grin at her. "You're sure a piece of work," he said, admiration warring with resentment in his mind. He couldn't bring himself to tell her he'd at least lived up to one personal commitment. And that had been to his grandmother. He'd had to watch her die a slow, terrible death, but he'd stayed by her side the whole time. That had been enough obligation to last him a lifetime.

Jane must have sensed some of his torment. Her hand

accidentally brushed against his then pulled back, but the feeling of her soft palm across his callused knuckles brought a flood of electric longing.

"We'll get through this together, Lenny. We're off to a good start. We'll do it gradually—just moving and sorting things. The idea is to keep what needs to be kept and get rid of the rest."

"Like ex-wives?" he asked with a wry grin.

"You're on a roll today, but yes, we might have to discuss how to handle that, too."

He thought if he could kiss her, he might be able to deal with a lot of things. "And how are we gonna handle that kiss we had the other day, Jane?"

She tried to pull away, but his hand held hers. "Jane?"

"That was just part of the deal, I think."

"Let's try it again and see."

She didn't say no. So he moved closer, reaching for her across the table. That didn't work, so he got up and pulled her into his arms, his mouth hitting on hers. For a while, they held together, the kiss channeling all the secrets Lenny couldn't voice. She loosened in his arms, feeling small and vulnerable and willing, so very willing.

Then she pulled away. "I don't think—"

Lenny didn't want her to think. But he said, "Okay, we won't think about this thing going on with us right now. I'm willing and able and apparently, I'm yours, Jane. I need your help. There, I said it. I want you to stay and help me. But I'm gonna need a lot of Steve Miller music playing in the background."

"Why do you listen to Steve Miller over and over?" she asked, her tone gentle, her mouth swollen and sexy.

Lenny almost turned grouchy again, only because he wanted to keep kissing her and only because she was putting that kiss right back in a safe place. Glancing around at the porcelain dolls sitting here and there in the clutter, he pushed away the pain of his memories.

"Before she died, Bertie stumbled across this old record collection I'd found in the attic—Steve Miller's very first single. That became one of her favorites. It's weird, but it seemed to soothe her—and the strangest part is that she used to hate it when I was young. Imagine my prim little grandmother suddenly liking classic rock and roll. We wore that one out and so I bought his greatest hits. She especially liked 'Take the Money and Run.'"

"Just part of the mystery of her disease," Jane said, her tone compassionate. "She probably liked the music because it kept her close to you. It made her feel safe. Even though she couldn't pinpoint the memories associated with it, it was familiar. And now that she's gone, the music—and these dolls—are your connections to her."

He had to swallow. He'd never cried after Bertie had died, but hearing that clinical observation made him want to let loose and howl tears of frustration and grief. Instead, he cleared his throat and shook his head. "That's really ironic, considering she used to tell me in her formal, polite way to turn it off."

"So you spent your teen years here?"

He nodded, ready to let go of some secrets. "I spent my life here from the time I was three years old. And that's all I have to say about that, doc."

Jane stood straight to stare at him. "You do realize that one day, you're going to need to talk about even that?"

He didn't speak. He just stood there, staring at the bright yellow mums spilling over in a vase on the kitchen table. Jane must have found them in the yard and picked some to grace the table. Thoughtful, was his little life coach.

Then Lenny looked from the mums to her. "Why are you doing this?"

She glanced at her notebook, her expression devoid of any trickery. And because Lenny was so used to trickery in women, that threw him completely. His body reacted to her earnest, honest expression as if he'd been sacked.

Jane put a hand on his and this time her touch was sure and precise. It was a simple gesture, but a deliberate one. It was the first time she'd touched him in any way of her own accord. And again, he felt winded and weak, tackled by one small feminine hand. Her fingers were warm and sure. But her words landed him, knocking his breath out of his body.

"Because you need me."

He was down. Blasted. Flattened.

Of all the women he'd ever known, not one of them had ever said that to him. They'd said all the right things at just the right moments, or so it had seemed at the time, but he couldn't ever remember a woman telling him that he needed her. They all always needed him, or wanted him for some purpose. As an escort who helped get their pictures in all the right magazines and society pages, as a lover who could help them ease their loneliness, as a friend who could have fun on an endless Saturday night, as a means unto an end—from getting some of his money or as a way to get some fancy jewelry, or maybe as a way to set themselves up in their own business, so they could get ahead of the game. Women always had a Plan B. But of all the women who had used him, abused him, loved him and left him, not one of them had ever said she was there because *Lenny* needed *her*. Maybe because he'd never felt he did need a woman. Until now.

And because this feeling was so new, so sharp-edged and raw, Lenny fought at it just as he'd always fought at anything and everything that caused him pain and anguish. He didn't want to analyze his feelings and he didn't want to be analyzed, not even by Jane. Certainly not by Jane. Not now. Maybe not ever.

He pushed away from the heat pouring between them, ignoring the pleading look in her eyes in the same way he was ignoring the plea shouting inside his heart. "I don't need anyone," he managed to say. "I'll go along with all your suggestions and I'll even talk to you, but I'm okay here. I was always okay here."

She gave him a skeptical look, but nodded, blessedly refraining from pushing him anymore. "I understand. I know how much you loved Bertie."

He turned, shaking his head. "No, you don't. Not at all. You didn't know her. You only know about what that disease did to her. But she sacrificed a lot for me. A whole lot."

"I'll do everything I can to protect and cherish your memories." She touched his arm again. "And I'll do everything I can to protect you." Then she closed her notebook. "Why don't we take a break and fix lunch?"

Normally, Lenny would have protested. But his shoulders ached from hoeing weeds this morning, and his mind was too full, too overflowing with the effort of keeping everything hidden away. And the effort of keeping Jane away when he wanted so much to draw her near.

He didn't want to think about all of this. So he thought of playing football. About how the shoulder pads and the uniform and the helmet helped to keep everything hidden away. About how he could call a few numbers and signals, then wait for the snap. He'd grab the ball and feel the smooth pigskin in his splayed hands, giving him control and power. He thought about lifting up, his muscles stretching and crunching as he looked out over the field. In spite of being focused and sure, he would hear the cheers and sneers of thousands of people while he surveyed the field, hoping to find the connection to victory. He couldn't drop the ball. That was the thing. He couldn't drop the ball. He'd rear back, his arm lifting, his mind centered on making that connection. Then, just before the hit, he'd send the ball spiraling through space, watching, waiting, praying.

And then he'd go down.

Sometimes, he managed to score points. Other times, he missed the running back's outstretched hands. But always, he felt safe, secure, covered, hidden, protected. Part of a team that surrounded him and aided him in reaching his goal.

He didn't like being open and exposed.

He liked being in control.

And in spite of Jane's best efforts, he knew that sooner or later, he was going to lose control. He was going to drop the ball. And after that, he didn't know.

He didn't want to know.

He didn't want to go down.

LATER THAT AFTERNOON, Jane strolled around the backyard, surveying what was left of the summer flowers, Boy running back and forth sniffing here and there in front of her.

Giant magnolia trees canopied each corner of the big sloping yard. Tall swaying pines hummed and danced in the fall wind. Azaleas, green and shimmering, would bloom again in the spring. And one sprawling dogwood hung suspended out near the white, wrought iron swing. It wasn't blooming now, either. But soon the clusters of winter camellias would fashion the garden with their fluffy pink flowers.

Boy surveyed every plant, trying some of them for relieving himself. Now the big dog plopped down near the swing, his eyes begging for someone to come and sit by him.

"Do you favor camellias?" Jane asked the dog as she walked toward the inviting swing. Boy only grunted, his big pink tongue hanging out one side of his mouth while she continued talking. "I love camellias." She eyed the many varieties in Bertie's garden. "My mother has several bushes growing in her yard up in Little Rock."

Boy whimpered a response that bordered on understanding.

Jane smiled down on the dog. He was growing on her, just like this place and this man were both growing on her. Lenny had kissed her again, there in the kitchen. And something had shifted and changed between them. They were no longer sparring or dealing or playing a game. This was serious.

To counter that heart-tugging admission, she focused on the garden. Most of the camellia bushes here looked old and well established, their lazy buds showing signs of the brilliant shades of pink that would range from light and cotton-candy colored to dark, passionate reddish-pink.

Then she glanced up to find Lenny standing across

the yard, staring at her. He stood there a minute then slowly walked toward her in an athletic gait that made her heart beat faster. Jane wanted to kiss him again, over and over.

But she stayed right where she was.

"Bertie planted these when she was a bride. That was over fifty years ago."

Jane nodded, careful to leave the questions for later. "They are certainly lovely."

He settled down beside her in the swing, one hand lifted toward a tall bush near the house. "Some are japonicas and some are sasanquas, so we get blooms almost all year long. That's an Angel. It blooms white." Then he waved toward a cluster near some tall pines. "Pink Perfection. And over there, Grand Prix." Then he pointed toward the pond. "And down there, my favorite. November Pink."

Jane tried to memorize each one, hoping she'd get to see them bloom again, especially the one Lenny had called his favorite. "November Pink. What a nice name for a flower."

"November's coming," Lenny said, his eyes going distant and vague. He shrugged. "And then winter."

Jane's heart shot forward with a sudden jolt as pretty golden oak leaves drifted by in the wind. She'd probably be back working at her office by November. "It won't be long now."

Lenny turned to stare at her, his eyes as crystal clear

as a mirror. "No, it won't be long now. And I guess by then I'll be all alone again."

Shocked that he wasn't just referring to the coming of winter, Jane wondered what Lenny was trying to say to her. "Are you all right?"

"I told you, Coach, I've always been fine here. Bertie used to tell me, 'He will not leave you comfortless.' I guess I just have to keep believing that, somehow."

Jane realized he was referring to God. There was little doubt that Lenny's grandmother had possessed a strong faith. Jane wondered if Lenny would be so strong when winter did come.

Then Lenny turned to her, reached for her hand, "Will you help me, Jane?"

Jane's heart hammered a resounding warning that pounded *no, no.* A warning that they were about to turn a corner, that Lenny had finally reached the point she'd been hoping for. But now she wasn't so sure *she* was ready. What could she say? "Of course," she answered, her tone muted. "That's why I'm here, Lenny. You know that."

He lowered his head, his breath tickling her ear, his lips just touching against her temple. "I don't like to talk about things. Can we not talk about things for a while?"

Jane didn't need a degree in psychology to understand Lenny's unresolved issues. But how in the world would she ever make him see that he did need to talk? To her.

Then she understood. In the process of putting his grandmother's house back in order, he would somehow open up to her, one memory at a time. It was the only way to handle this man. "We don't have to talk until you're ready."

As she allowed Lenny to hold her hand and gently rock the swing, Jane realized this was going to be her toughest assignment yet. Because she was breaking a big rule. She was beginning to care way too much about her client. And even that old mutt, Boy, too.

CHAPTER TEN

"WE'LL GET A BITE to eat after the game," Lenny told Jane as they pulled into the stadium. "Since it's a school night, the kids can't go out for pizza. I'll treat them at the next practice if we win. And we will win." Then the need to tease her kicked in. "Oh, and you'll probably be the talk of the game. People will think you're my date."

"Am I your date?" she asked, never skipping a beat.

"Heck, no. I mean, yes, maybe." He looked down to see an impish smile cresting her face. "You just said that to get next to me, didn't you?"

"Maybe. Did it work?"

Lenny managed a chuckle. "You're full of surprises, aren't you?"

"I have to be with a man like you."

Lenny didn't know whether to laugh or cry at that smug remark. He needed to remember how smart this woman was. Come to think of it, he'd never been attracted to smart before. But he sure was with Jane. It was disturbing in a refreshing kind of way.

TWO HOURS LATER, Jane could fully understand why Lenny Paxton no longer had the desire to walk the red carpet or be in the spotlight. He was having fun coaching little boys in football. He was still involved in the game without taking another risk. And maybe that was healthy in a weird kind of way.

"Thanks for inviting me," she said as they were leaving. "That was fun."

"Hang with me, doc, and you'll always have fun," he retorted with a wicked grin.

The Warthogs had won 7-0 and Lenny had promised the boys pizza Friday night. Jane laughed at his antics, then glanced back. "I think people are wondering who I am. Everyone treated me like some sort of strange bug, looking but never getting too close."

Lenny shook his head. "Oh, they all know who you are, Miss Jane Harper. Everyone in town is talking about the life coach—and probably Wanda's unique styling tactic, too. I'm pretty sure they're still placing bets on how long you'll stick around. Or how long before you're head over heels for me, of course."

"I've been in worse situations," she retorted, choosing to ignore his confidence or her self-consciousness regarding that confidence, while he opened the Corvette passenger-side door for her. The man had several nice automobiles stashed away in the old barn. "Okay, maybe the hog pen was the worst yet, but I survived it."

"Yeah, well, I'm not sure that old bull hog will ever get over it." He turned, gripping the wheel as he stared over at her. "You know, you're cute in an adorable academic way. It was nice to see you up there in the stands. You made me feel safe for some strange reason."

Jane didn't know how to respond to that. So she sat silent while he backed the car up and zoomed up the gravel lane, taking them away from the football field. The cool September wind hit her face as the convertible picked up speed. She had to admit being with Lenny made her feel safe, too. But this was a working relationship, no matter how good he looked in worn jeans and a T-shirt with a snarling red hog on the front.

Trying to get back to business, she asked, "Do you think you'll ever leave the farm again? I mean, once we've cleared your head?"

He ran a hand through his thick hair, but remained silent. Jane placed her hands together in her lap. She noted his taut jaw, his hand clutching the gear stick. And she also saw his pain. The man had lost someone close to him and he'd lost a big game—the game of his career. Now he'd lost his confidence, too. And maybe his drive.

"I don't know, Coach. I...I get all sweaty and my heart starts pounding if I go past the city limit sign."

That confession floored her. But instead of her usual inclination at such a breakthrough, which would have been to push more, she reached over and touched his hand. "Then we won't go past that sign until you're ready. So where are you taking me tonight?"

"I think you'll like this place," Lenny said, smiling the smile of a man who'd just been given a reprieve.

Why did the man's smile make her all warm and gooey inside? She didn't do warm and gooey. She was starving but her nerves were a bit frazzled and her allergies had her sniffing and sneezing. She'd taken an allergy pill before the game and now she felt lethargic. That was the only explanation for why she'd refrained from launching into a discussion about his apparent anxiety attacks. Maybe some good food would perk her up and get her back on task.

"I'm hungry," she said over the wind that poured around them in the convertible.

"Good. The seafood is the best," he said, his grin making her go from warm to gooey to downright loopy.

He looked so young and carefree tonight. Focusing on that, Jane mentally patted herself on the back. Maybe she truly was making a difference with Lenny. "Well, we certainly deserve a good meal," she replied. "We worked hard today and your team won."

He let out a hoot and shifted gears as the car moved like a sleek cat up the winding country road. All around them, fall leaves whirled and danced, the woods a lush gold in the tail end of a brilliant sunset. And Steve Miller sang "Fly Like an Eagle" on the CD.

"We sure did. And I have to admit, it feels good getting that kitchen in order." Then he put a hand on hers, causing Jane to turn toward those incredible blue eyes.

"It looks like Bertie's kitchen again and for that, I thank you."

"We did it together." She didn't pull away, which would have been her first inclination a few days ago. "What?" she asked, happy at the way he kept glancing at her, his eyes smiling a secret.

"You," he said. "You managed to help me get the kitchen all spick-and-span and you didn't once suggest I throw anything away."

"But you did throw a few things away," she said, glowing from his praise. "It's not my job to decide what goes and what stays. That's your decision. I'm just there to guide you."

"To coach me, you mean."

The way he said things—Jane got all mushy again. "Yes, to coach you. Bertie's kitchen is intact and her memory is still there but now you have a place to work without clutter and chaos. You can honor her memories."

"She'd be so proud." Then he squeezed Jane's hand. "She would have loved you."

Trying not to let that sweet compliment go to her already spinning head, Jane nodded. "I take it Bertie was a neat freak, too?"

He downshifted as they turned onto yet another long mountain road. "She liked order, yes. She was a lot like you—precise, organized. She made lists and schedules, mainly because she was a schoolteacher for so many years. And she had to keep up with me."

Jane refrained from clapping. She didn't want him to realize he was actually talking about the past. "I can tell from what's underneath all the mess that she loved her home."

He pulled the purring car into a graveled parking lot in front of a long cabin-type building. "I'm ashamed I let things get so bad."

Jane knew she couldn't push him. "Well, we're going to get that house back into shape and we're going to get you past the county line."

He let go of her hand then switched off the car. "I'm beginning to believe that."

Jane got out of the car before he could come around and open her door. She'd dressed carefully in jeans and a light blue cashmere sweater, hoping she didn't look as prim and uptight as Lenny seemed to think she was. And her insides were changing, shifting into something that wasn't at all familiar to her. Not keyed up, but anxious all the same. But this was a good kind of anticipation. Was she going soft? Or was she truly learning how to relax?

"You look nice," he said, as if he could see the doubts in her eyes.

He didn't look too shabby either, Jane noted, taking in that ridiculously cute Warthog shirt. "Thanks. I'm a little nervous about this setup. You know, you coaching me. Exactly what will you be coaching me in again? I know how to eat and I know how to laugh."

"Do you really know how to have a good time?" he

asked, a finger hot on her open lips. "Let me be your guide tonight. I did my part this afternoon. And as a way to thank you for sticking with me, I want to treat you to a nice dinner. Nothing more, okay?"

"Okay," she said as he took her by the hand, "but I never said I can't have fun."

He grinned down at her just as they stepped on the long porch of the Ozark Sunset Restaurant. "You didn't have to say anything," he replied.

Jane didn't like that comment. She'd show Lenny Paxton she could loosen up. It's just that she rarely had time to explore that side of her personality.

After a cute waitress seated them at a rustic table on the back porch, Jane settled into her comfortable cane-backed chair and stared out at the lake. It was a cool fall night, but pleasant and calm. "I see how this place got its name."

Lenny followed her gaze out to where the last rays of the sun seemed to be floating just above the burnished water and trees. "Yep. This is the best view on this old mountain. You can't beat this."

"Do they always give you the best seat in the house?" she asked. "I saw the way everyone took notice when we walked in."

"They know me here, yeah." His grin was pure male and completely magnetic. "I guess being a has-been has its perks."

"Don't call yourself that," she admonished. "You're just at a different place in your life now."

"Yeah, like a standstill." He leaned back, his gaze sweeping over her face. "And until you showed up, I thought that's exactly where I wanted to be. I should be angry that you've forced me to look at my situation, but tonight I'm just sad about some things and happy about others."

"You're grieving, Lenny. Anyone can see that."

"When does it end?" he asked, his question low and for her ears only, his eyes dancing with doubt.

"I don't think it ever ends," she said, trying to be honest. "I've never lost anyone close, but I've counseled lots of clients who have. And I can tell you that things would have only gotten worse if I hadn't intervened. A cluttered house is about so much more than just being disorganized."

"Tell me about you, Jane," he said, his tone indicating he'd had enough of the clutter issues. "Tell me about your family."

She figured this was a stalling tactic, but she went along with it only because he was beginning to trust her with little tidbits of what made him tick.

"I have two sisters and a brother. We're large and loud, everyone is opinionated but we love each other. I've always lived on or near a college campus and it was a given that I'd just naturally attend the University of Arkansas. I'm the oldest, so I suppose that makes me the consummate overachiever."

Lenny nodded as she spoke. "Sounds like a good

family. I've often wondered what it would be like to have a brother or sister."

Jane had to bite back the questions zooming through her mind, but she ached for him. He was alone in this world, in spite of all the people who shadowed him. "Being in a big family has good and bad moments. It's odd, but we're not an overly demonstrative family. We're not touchy-feely. But we fight for each other, no questions asked."

His eyes went dark then he looked out at the lake. "That's a nice feeling, having someone to fight for you. Bertie was always my champion."

"And then you were hers, in the end."

"Let's change the subject." He gave her that killer grin again. "And maybe my first lesson after this dinner should be showing you how to be a little more touchy-feely, know what I mean?"

The shiver sliding down her backbone knew exactly what he meant. She took a long drink of the water their waitress had sat down on the table. "Uh, I don't think—"

"That's just it," Lenny said, holding his glass up. "Don't think. That's the first rule of the Lenny Paxton way of coaching. Don't think."

Jane shook her head. "I can't *not* think. I have to analyze everything."

"Shh," he said. "Let's pick out what we want to eat. One step at a time, right, Coach?"

"Right." Jane couldn't argue with his logic. And she

had to admit it felt good—odd and strange and foreign, but good—to have a handsome man flirting with her. "I think I'll have the blackened catfish."

"Good choice." Lenny motioned the waitress over and ordered a steak medium-rare. "And don't forget dessert," he said. "They have the best pie around."

The waitress bobbed her head. "Sure do. We get them fresh from Barbara's Baked Goods."

Jane let out a gasp after the waitress sauntered away. "Figures at least one of your ex-wives would somehow be involved in this meal."

Lenny looked uncomfortable then smiled. "Uh, make that two. My third ex-wife kind of owns this place." Then he turned as he heard a commotion coming from the kitchen, his skin going pale. After muttering something underneath his breath, he said, "And here she comes right now."

Jane looked up to find a healthy blonde, no, make that an Amazon woman wearing cowboy boots, tight jeans and a big grin, coming toward their table. "You brought me to a restaurant that your third ex-wife owns?"

Lenny's tanned face went from pale to two shades darker. "Yes, because the food's good, and I thought she was out of town."

But Jane was beyond believing him. Too hurt to think straight and too woozy from her allergy pill to be coherent, she asked, "Is this another one of your little tricks?"

"It's not like that," Lenny said, reaching for her.

Jane recoiled as if he were a rattlesnake. And he was a snake. A snake in the grass, tricking her, laughing at her, kissing her and flirting with her in front of all his infernal ex-wives. It was silly, but it felt like high school and college all over again. A jock teasing her. Embarrassing her.

"I'm leaving," she said, getting up only to find the Amazon woman staring down at her.

"Hey, there," the woman said, one hand on her hip. "How're y'all?"

Lenny stood, too, giving Jane a look that begged forgiveness. "Uh, Tiffany, I thought you were in Broken Bow."

"I got home early," Tiffany said, running a hand over her spiked blond locks, her vivid green eyes centered on Jane. "Candy called me. And from the look of things, not a minute too soon, either."

LENNY WANTED to drop through the porch. How could he have been so stupid? Now Jane was fuming and hurt and Tiffany was doing the toe-tap that all of his ex-wives had a habit of doing when they were extremely upset with him—or having a laugh on him.

He turned to Jane, but in her usual take-charge way, she went into a steamroller kind of calm. "Hi, I'm Jane Harper, the life coach. I'm sure Candy told you all about me. But just in case she didn't give you the whole scoop, go ahead and insult me. Then you can ask me anything you want to know, but before you do, I can assure you that I'm here in a strictly professional manner and that I don't have the hots for your ex-husband. In fact, right now, I truly feel sorry for the man."

Tiffany stood back, her hand out. "Whoa, there, honey. Slow down before you hyperventilate." Turning to Lenny, she asked, "Is she always like this?"

"Pretty much," Lenny said, grabbing Jane by the arm. "Jane, this is Tiffany Warner."

"The third ex-wife," Jane said, her eyes going glassy. She seemed flushed. Was she really about to hyperventilate? "So nice to meet you, *Tiffany*."

She said that name with such disdain, Lenny gave her a warning look as he tried to smooth things over. "I'm sorry, Tiff. I wouldn't have come here if I'd known—"

Tiffany started laughing, really loud. "Shoot, honey, I'm used to seeing you with other women." She gave Jane a long, hard, green-eyed stare. "Not exactly cheerleader type, but I guess she just might do."

Jane squirmed, trying to get away from Lenny. "And I suppose you *were* a cheerleader at some point in your life, right?"

Tiffany laughed even harder. "I sure was, but hey, I just joined the team to meet football players. Of course, that didn't get me anywhere until years later when I was an NFL cheerleader and I met Lenny." She tossed Lenny a glance. "Come to think of it, *that* didn't get me anywhere either."

"It…uh…didn't work out," Lenny tried to explain.

"Amen to that," Tiffany countered. "It didn't work on oh so many levels."

"I get that," Jane said, taking a long, shuddering breath. "It's nice to meet you, Tiffany."

Tiffany clapped her hands together. "I do believe Candy and Barbara were right about you two."

Lenny saw his hopes for the night sinking right along with the red-hot sunset. "Y'all have discussed us?"

"Sure we have," Tiffany said, wiping tears of mirth from her eyes. "We expected Jane to show up and have some fun with us this afternoon. Candy said she'd invited her, but I guess your life coach was tied up or something."

Jane bristled so fast at the implications of that remark, Lenny felt the red-hot charge moving like lightning through his hand on her arm. "We've been trying to straighten out things around the farm."

Tiffany slanted her head, her dangling gold earrings shimmying. "Yeah, right." She winked at Jane. "Well, good luck with trying to straighten out this smooth-talker, suga'."

Jane looked from Tiffany to Lenny, then with quick efficiency, yanked her arm away from Lenny's grip. He expected her to march right out of the restaurant, but instead she smiled so sweetly at Tiffany he stepped back, a bad feeling settling like an apple wedge inside his gut.

Then Jane sat down. "I'll have a margarita."

"On the rocks or frozen?" Tiffany replied, not nearly as shocked as Lenny.

"On the rocks," Jane replied, waving a hand at Tiffany in a firm dismissal. "And could you please bring some bread. I'm starving."

"Yes, ma'am." Tiffany gave a smug little salute then turned to do Jane's bidding.

"We can leave," Lenny said, slowly easing back into his chair so as not to ruffle her feathers.

"Why?" Her smile was beautiful, but deadly. "After all, you said the food here is wonderful. And you owe me a meal, remember?"

"Yes, but I thought…"

Jane leaned forward, brushing a long strand of burnished hair away from her face. Except she missed one luscious strand that caught on her flushed cheekbone, leaving Lenny with images of rich silk.

"Oh, I know what you thought. You thought I'd lose my temper and storm out of here, right? You had to make one last effort to drive me away, didn't you, Lenny? And in spite of all we've accomplished over the last few days." Her voice went to a whisper. "In spite of the trust I've tried so hard to build with you. I thought we'd made some progress but you were just stringing me along. You kissed me, but I guess that wasn't real either, was it?"

Lenny hated the hurt and defeat in her voice. Did he dare tell her just how real that kiss had felt?

"We have made process, doc," he said, stuttering in

his haste to make her see. "You know that, Jane. You have to believe me."

"I don't believe anything that comes out of your mouth," she said, her smile icy. "But I'm here to tell you that if you try one more stunt like this, you will live to regret it, Lenny. Do you understand me?"

"Yes, ma'am," he said, sitting back in defeat, his insides sizzling with the heat of that sweet declaration. "I'm sorry. I really wanted tonight to be special."

A waitress brought steaming bread and a frosty margarita. Jane bypassed the bread and downed half the drink.

"Hey, take it slow," Lenny told her. "Tiffany makes a mean margarita."

Jane ignored him, then grabbed a piece of bread and buttered it with precision, her eyes gleaming as she moved the knife back and forth over the crisp toast. "I'll bear that in mind. I'm really surprised that between the three of them, I haven't been poisoned in my sleep. Your wives are very territorial."

"Ex-wives," he reminded her. "They haven't quite learned to let go, I reckon."

"You think?" She shoved bread into her mouth, chewing it in a choppy, noisy way while her eyes chewed him into pieces. "I think it's a bit odd that they all hang around you, waiting like a harem for handouts. It's kind of pathetic when you think about it."

Lenny couldn't argue with that. "I guess I'm the one

who can't let go. I feel responsible for all of them. I want to make sure they're all okay."

She nodded, chewed some more, drank some more. "And I bet you're a silent partner in this restaurant and that you invested heavily in Barbara's Baked Goods and that you own stock in a couple of shoe stores just to keep Candy happy. You probably even financed Wanda's street front beauty salon, too, since she seems destined to be wife number four."

He winced, answer enough that she got the message.

"Just as I thought," she said on a soft hiss, bread crumbs blowing out around her cute mouth.

"Wanda needed help. I couldn't turn her down."

"Of course not. You're so very noble that way."

Trying to get the ball back into possession, he sat up then grinned. "You know, if I didn't know better I'd think you're just a wee bit jealous, Coach."

She finished her drink then held up the glass to signal for another. "That is ridiculous. I do find it tedious the way women keep coming out of the woodwork to bask in the glow of your charms. But then, I guess that's part of the package."

"There is no package," he said, hoping to steer things back around to having a nice, quiet dinner. "I'm just me. Plain and simple and…confused right now."

"I can understand the confused part," she retorted with a tad too much sympathy for Lenny's liking. "But there is nothing plain and simple about you, that's for sure. More subject matter for me to analyze. We've cleaned your kitchen, but it might take a lot longer to clean all that clutter out of your head."

Lenny was about to give her a retort of his own when a funny thing happened. She dropped her piece of bread, her face going flush again, her pupils dilating. "I don't feel so hot," she managed to mumble. "I normally don't drink very much, hardly ever, really."

Then she tried to stand up.

Lenny saw her wobble then sway. He jumped up to come around the small table. "Jane?"

She gave him a look full of fear and shock then reached out toward him. Lenny caught her in his arms just before she hit the floor.

LENNY CARRIED Jane straight out the door, too mortified and worried to look back. He made it to the Corvette and managed to get the door open before she started moaning.

"Let me go," she said, her voice low.

"You drank too much, too fast," he said, wishing he'd stopped her. Wishing he'd stopped all of this.

She lifted her arm in the air, almost hitting him square in the eyes with her wayward thrashing. "I don't drink."

"I never would have guessed that."

He got her in her seat belt then headed around the car. Then he heard Tiffany calling after him.

"Hey, Lenny, wait up!"

"Not now, Tiffany. You've done enough damage for one night. You put too much liquor in that drink." He got in and backed up, spewing gravel.

But he'd forgotten that besides being a cheerleader, Tiffany had also run track in college. She caught up with him as he tried to turn out of the drive.

"Her purse, Lenny," she called, not even breathing hard as she hit a hand on the car. "You left her purse."

Lenny stopped to reach for the big bag, intent on making a quick getaway. But Tiffany's hand on the steering wheel stopped him. "This fell out."

Lenny stared down at the prescription bottle, his heart pounding faster than a rusher blocking a play. "What is that?"

"Some kind of allergy pill," Tiffany said. "I didn't add anything to her drink. She must have taken one of these and I guess it didn't mix well with the tequila."

Lenny hit the steering wheel. "Well, now, isn't that just wonderful. I have plans for a romantic dinner and between the three of us, we messed this night up to beat the band."

Tiffany eyed Jane then looked back at Lenny. "I think she'll be okay if you let her sleep it off. But I'm worried about you."

Lenny decided then and there that he really was tired of women worrying about him. "I'm fine. Now let me get her checked out at the emergency room."

"You're not so fine, sweetie," Tiffany said through a chuckle. "I do believe you've met your match."

Lenny turned to where Jane lay crumbled against the leather seat, her hair covering her face like a burnished burgundy streaked blanket. She looked so sweet and vulnerable, all quiet and passed out like that. "I don't know what you're talking about and I have to go."

"Oh, you know," Tiffany replied. "You're falling in love, Lenny. Maybe for the fourth or fifth time." She tapped her hand on the car then lifted away. "Or maybe for the very first time."

CHAPTER ELEVEN

LENNY SAT in the waiting room rubbing his hands together. When the double doors to the emergency room opened, he shot up out of his chair, almost tackling the young doctor in his haste to find out if Jane was okay.

"She's fine," the doctor said with a hand in the air. "A bad mix of tequila and strong sinus pills, just as you thought. Good thing she only had the one drink."

"Can I take her home?" Lenny asked, afraid to face Jane. She was probably fit to be tied.

"Yes. Make sure you put her to bed and let her sleep it off. She'll be a little groggy tomorrow, but she'll be all right. You were wise to bring her in. It's never good to mix medicine with liquor."

Lenny didn't trust doctors anymore. "You're sure?"

"I'm sure," the doctor said. He turned to leave but pivoted at the doors. "Oh, one of the nurses wanted your autograph, Mr. Paxton. She'll be bringing Ms. Harper out any minute now."

Lenny nodded, his mind on anything but giving out an autograph. He waited, pacing back and forth, until he heard the doors opening again. A perky blond nurse wheeled a bleary-eyed, slumped-shouldered Jane through the doors. Lenny ignored the nurse, instead taking in Jane's tangled hair, her red-rimmed, glazed eyes and the way she hung onto the arms of the wheelchair.

Stopping in front of him, the nurse handed him a note pad. "Sign here, please." Lenny signed, not even noticing if it was an official document or not. "And… uh…here." The nurse handed him a picture of a baby. "It's my son, Jack. I want him to have your autograph. Who knows, maybe one day he'll be in the NFL, too."

Lenny impatiently scrawled his name at the bottom of the picture. "Can we get out of here now?"

The nurse appeared disappointed, but nodded. "You're free to go."

He leaned down to face Jane. "I'm taking you home, okay?"

"I never got dinner," she said in a small voice, her lips just beyond a quiver. "Some hot date you are."

"I'll find us something to eat," he replied as he ignored hospital policy and scooped her out of the wheelchair to carry her out the doors and to his car. She obediently laid her head on his shoulder and wrapped her sweet little arms around his neck, a soft sigh coming from deep inside her. Lenny shifted her slight weight. She was so fragile, so delicate, he was afraid he might break her. But she was also buff and firm, with an underlying core that signified just how strong this tiny woman really was. He hated himself for what he'd done to her. He had wanted tonight to be different.

She shifted, burrowing closer. "You're warm. So warm."

Lenny got warmer by the minute. He stopped midway to the car, just to stare down at her face. Her cute innocent little face. How had this woman stayed that way, all trusting and pure and almost gullible? And why did it seem as if he'd just now discovered what a real woman was all about—part innocence and part strength all rolled into one bundle of pure feminine allure. His heart opened like a penalty flag fluttering in the wind while he stared down into Jane's heart-shaped face. He might have to drop back and punt on this one.

He wanted to say so much, but he figured she wouldn't remember anything he said, or if she did, she wouldn't believe any of it anyway. Instead, he settled her into the car, buckling her up, and then got in beside her to work at bringing the top up.

"Leave it down," she said, her head resting at an angle against her seat, her left arm going up in a wobbly protest. "I need some fresh air."

Lenny did as she asked then drove off into the night, intent on getting her safely home and all tucked in before he did something really crazy like kiss her silly.

"I'M SORRY, JANE."

Jane's mind swirled with voices and lights. She couldn't quite remember where she was or why she was here.

She felt strong arms lifting her, a warmth surrounding

her and cushioning her. She inhaled the spice of the sea and the wind mixed with a distinctive male presence. She heard a man's voice inside her head, saying the same words over and over.

"I'm sorry, Jane."

Lenny.

Jane opened her eyes. She was in the tiny den toward the back of Bertie's house. The den by the sleeping porch that served as a kind of office-workout room for Lenny.

Lenny.

It all came tumbling back then in bits and pieces. The allergy pill, the restaurant, the sunset, the third ex-wife. The tequila.

"Let me up," she said, trying to sit. But her head swirled again, spinning out of control. "Uh, oh…" She sank back down underneath the chenille blanket, pulling it up over her eyes to make the swirling stop.

"It's okay. You're okay now. Just rest."

Lenny's voice soothed her even while it grated on her nerves. She wanted to be mad at him, but that wasn't very professional. Nothing about this had been professional. She'd messed everything up. Everything. She'd come here, all high-handed and smug, intent on straightening out the great Lenny Paxton while she profited from her time here by selling her story to that stupid *Sidelined* magazine.

Now, she didn't want to write an exclusive story on Lenny. She *couldn't* sell what had happened here.

Because she couldn't get past how he'd kissed her and made her feel alive—and all the while he'd been setting her up for a great fall. Well, she'd fallen all right.

And she'd failed. Miserably.

"Hey, you want something to eat now?"

"No. Go away."

He tugged at the fringe hiding her face. "I made coffee."

She could smell it. Maybe coffee would help. "Okay."

She heard the tap of his boots hitting the worn wooden floor. Wouldn't these lovely old floors be so pretty, sanded and polished and shined up? Wouldn't this house be great when they got it back into shape?

Why am I here? Jane wondered, a heavy morose feeling settling around her on the old, butter-soft leather sofa. Opening one eye, she surveyed the clutter. This room, which had been off limits to her until now, was way too small for all the things Lenny had tossed into it. This house was way too full of angst and sadness for any one man to try and live here. It truly was depressing.

You're here for Lenny, she reminded herself. *He needs to toss out a few things. He doesn't want you here. He's trying to toss you away, too. Don't take it personally.*

But it was personal.

She sat up, her mind whirling with conflicting thoughts that involved Good Lenny and Bad Lenny. Between the combination of the alcohol and medicine, Jane's mind was all fuzzy and tangled. It felt as if she'd been caught in a giant spiderweb and she couldn't break free. "I have to get a handle on this," she told herself in a firm little voice.

Then she slumped back down. Tomorrow. She'd figure it all out tomorrow.

LENNY CAME BACK with the coffee only to find her sleeping. "Jane?"

She didn't answer and she didn't move. So he sat down and took a sip of the hot brew, enjoying the darkness and the midnight quiet and the sound of her steady, sure breathing.

Then he remembered sitting in this very room next to a hospital bed, watching and listening as Bertie breathed her last breath. And with that last breath, his grandmother who'd protected him and raised him, had also taken the delicate web of tangled memories she'd unknowingly shared about his long-dead mother. He'd lost both of them, all over again. It all came back to him in a brilliant flash of pain and longing, and just like that, he wanted it all to go away. He wanted this house clean and pretty again. He wanted his life to be back on track again. He wanted to start over.

With Jane.

Shocked at that realization, he leaned forward to put his coffee cup on top of a ragged stack of magazines on the side table. *Sports Illustrated* muscled in on *Cottage Crafts*. He put his head in his hands, trying to push at the tears spilling from his eyes. The great rush of emotions filled him like a rain-covered field of torn wet grass and gushing dirty mud. And then he understood how long he'd been holding all this inside, how long he'd been collecting clutter to cover up everything that was broken inside his heart.

"Lenny?"

From somewhere inside the fog choking off his breath, Lenny heard Jane calling his name.

He lifted his head to find her eyes open and centered on him. "Lenny?" And then she opened her arms wide.

He sat there, dumbfounded and paralyzed. It had been such a long time since a woman had offered him any kind of consolation. Maybe because he'd always managed to hold them all at arm's length. He'd measured every relationship as if he were trying to advance his team down the field to score. And once he had scored the pretty woman, the devoted wife, the prize on his arm, he'd lost all the fight of the battle. Only to realize he wasn't happy.

But now, right this minute, in the midst of all his pain and fear and torment and triumph, Jane still made him smile. She made him smile because she had been, from the start, willing to fight for him. Not against him, not with him. But for him. And for some strange, unexplainable reason, that made Lenny very happy. A healing kind of happy that gave him such a burst of energy and relief and awakening, he couldn't contain it.

Lenny got up, wiping his eyes as he stumbled toward her. Without saying a word, Jane took him into her arms to pull him down on the sofa beside her. "It's okay, Lenny. I'm here. I'm here."

"I don't want to talk," he managed to whisper, his lips searching for hers.

"You don't have to," she said, touching a hand to his face. Then she kissed his face and finally, his lips, her touch as sweet and healing as a gentle rain. And his lust turned to longing. Lifting away to give him a lopsided smile, she pulled the spread up over both of them then settled into his arms.

Lenny held her close as she fell back asleep, realizing for the first time in his life that true relationships were about a lot more than just physical pleasure. This time, his heart was right there caught up in Jane's arms. And he wanted to keep it that way.

JANE WOKE UP to bright sunlight shining through the windows on the adjoining sunporch by the den. Her head felt weighted and heavy, her pulse pounding with each movement she made. She blinked, thinking she was having such a nice dream. In her dream, this tiny room was now neat and orderly and clean. She blinked again, opening her eyes wide to make sure she was seeing right.

The little office den *was* clean and tidy. Wondering how Lenny had managed that without waking her, she glanced around to make sure one more time. The workout equipment was still in the corner but now clear of the dirty T-shirts and old towels. The tables, once covered with old issues of sports magazines and newspapers mixed in with knitting magazines and gardening books, were now clean except for the dainty white doilies that had been hidden underneath. The bookshelves still held books, but they were neat and in order, easy to find. And the floor, once covered with books, DVDs, clothes and equipment, was swept tidy. The room looked a lot bigger now. And it looked happy.

"I really need coffee," she said, wondering if she was dreaming the smell of bacon, too. In spite of her aching head, she was starving. And curious about what had made him clean up all around her. Especially after she'd fallen asleep holding him. He'd held her right back, tightly, gently, completely. Jane's heart burned with that memory, even if her brain was still fuzzy.

"Note to self—never again drink a margarita...or two—after taking a heavy-duty allergy pill," she said as she stumbled to the kitchen, expecting to find Lenny waiting there for her.

Last night was still out of focus, but she was pretty sure Lenny had experienced some sort of breakthrough sitting there while she slept. Then she remembered that he'd held her there on the couch for part of the night. She had other memories, too. Memories of her face pressed against his shoulder, of his lips grazing her cheeks, memories of his kisses. Maybe she'd just dreamed that part. She must have slept like the dead for him to have worked around her.

"That smells so good," she said, glancing up, ready to commend him on his hard work.

Barbara stood at the stove, looking as prim and proper in a print dress and dainty apron as she'd looked the first time Jane had met her.

"Uh, where's Lenny?"

Barbara whirled with spatula in hand. "Oh, he's checking on those infernal hogs. And he wanted to water the garden. I declare if we don't get some rain around here—"

Ignoring the weirdness of Barbara's too-happy conversation, Jane didn't like the sound of this. Lenny had obviously left before she woke up, probably because he was embarrassed about last night. So in an effort to put yet another buffer between them, he'd called in reinforcements. Ex-wife number two.

"Are we alone?" Jane asked, glancing around as she pushed at her disheveled hair.

Barbara beamed a smile. "Yes. Candy's still at my house, but she doesn't get up till noon and Tiffany had to supervise the breakfast crowd at the restaurant, since it's a fine Saturday morning. And I told Henry he didn't have to come by this morning."

"Good. A reprieve," Jane replied, grasping for a cup.

Barbara handed her one, full of steaming coffee. "Drink up. Lenny told me what happened."

Jane wanted to ask if he'd told her *everything* that

had happened, but she didn't. Her memories of last night were still too muted and dreamlike to be sure.

"I've made pancakes and bacon," Barbara said, motioning to Jane to sit down. "And dry toast, if you'd rather have that. I'm off to clean Bertie's room."

"The room I'm staying in?" Jane said as she held the hot coffee cup to her temple in an effort to stop the throbbing in her brain.

Barbara pulled the aspirin bottle out of a cabinet. "Here, take this with some orange juice." She produced the orange juice in a jiffy, handing the flower-bordered glass to Jane.

Jane downed the aspirin and juice then chased it with a long gulp of coffee. "You don't have to clean my room, Barbara."

"Oh, it's okay. I clean Bertie's room at least once a month. Lenny insists on that."

Jane sank down, wondering how many more surprises she'd have to get through before she got to the real Lenny Paxton. "But why?"

Barbara buffed the clean counter. "Well, because…it's Bertie's room. He wouldn't let me clean this kitchen—looks so good now by the way—and he refuses to let me touch any other part of the house. Just her room."

"Did she…die in that room?"

"No, she died in the room down the hall—Lenny's office now. When she got real bad, he put a hospital bed in there so she could see out into the garden. And he slept on the couch or the sleeping porch most nights. Still sleeps there a lot I think."

Jane absorbed this information like a sponge. No wonder he'd had that meltdown last night. He'd been forced to come face-to-face with his grandmother's death, having to sit there and nurse Jane during the night. And now, in the light of day, he couldn't face things.

He couldn't face her.

Barbara dried her hands on a rooster-encased dish towel. "He's never allowed anyone in Bertie's room. Until you."

Jane refused to get excited about that. "Probably because it was clean," she reasoned.

"Or maybe he wanted you to see this house the way it once was," Barbara replied. "The man can't see the forest for the trees most days."

"How did you two wind up together?" Jane asked as she nibbled on a fluffy pancake.

"Pie," Barbara said, plain and simple. "Of course, as good as it is for a lot of things, pie can't sustain a marriage."

"I guess not," Jane replied. Although one of Barbara's pies would certainly come close to doing the trick. Curious, she touched a hand to her coffee mug. "Why is it that all of you cling to Lenny, and why is it that his other two exes like to stay at your house?"

Barbara sat down across from Jane, her blue eyes sweet with sincerity. "Well, my house belongs to

Lenny—I mean he gave it to me as part of our divorce settlement. We built it together but then when things fell apart, he knew I loved that house. So he let me stay there. I think he wanted someone nearby after Albert died, to help out with Bertie. You know, check on her, take her to church and to the doctor." She shrugged. "I love it here. And as for Candy and Tiffany, we kinda got to be friends out of our love and concern for Lenny, I reckon."

"Just like that?"

"Oh, no. It took a while for all of us to come to terms. You see, we each thought we'd be the one he'd take back."

"Lenny might not be capable of ever settling down with one woman," Jane said, trying to be reasonable.

"Oh, I think he might. If he finds the right woman."

"You mean, a combination of all of you, maybe?"

"No," Barbara said, her laughter tinkling like chimes. "I mean, a woman so different from the lot of us that she just presents too much of a challenge for him, at exactly the time he needs her to challenge him." She gave Jane a sweetly resigned look.

Jane shook her head. "You don't mean—"

"I do so," Barbara said on a little sigh. "I saw that man this morning, Jane. He was determined to get that room clean before you woke up. He kept saying—whispering really—he was doing it for you. For Jane. And the way he said that, well, let me tell you—I've never seen Lenny

Paxton so surefire determined." She touched a hand to her hair then lowered her voice. "You've managed to do in a week what the rest of us tried for years. Find his heart."

"He's not doing this for me," Jane explained. "He's finally getting to the bottom of his issues and his grief. Last night brought it all to the surface."

"Whatever he's getting to, you're sure getting to him," Barbara replied. "It's nice to see him being constructive and disciplined for a change."

"I have to go and talk to him," Jane said, finishing up the last of her pancakes and bacon. She dreaded it, but she had to confess about that magazine article that she was so not going to write. "This breakfast was great. Thanks."

"I'll miss this," Barbara said. "I come over and cook for him once or twice a week. I guess that will have to stop."

"Why? You aren't moving away, are you?"

"Not if Lenny will let me stay on after—"

"After he's better, you mean. Why would he want you to move?"

Barbara just smiled. "We'll cross that bridge when we come to it, honey."

Reminding herself that the conversations around here could be cryptic at times, Jane nodded. "I'm going to change clothes then I'm going to find Lenny. Two rooms down and about four to go. But we're making progress."

"Yes, you are," Barbara said. Then she started stacking dishes, humming as she went.

JANE WALKED THE PERIMETER of the property, the cool morning breeze soothing her frazzled nerve-endings as she stretched her muscles and inhaled clean country air. She was awake and aware as the cold air sizzled and hummed around her. Something about a crisp fall morning made her feel good in spite of her hangover.

A giant sycamore tree just off the trail shimmered in the slow-moving wind, its big leaves dropping like ballerinas dancing in a graceful spiraling swirl to the ground. She came up on one of the old barns, surprised to find it there all red and gray and cracked. But it looked right, settled back against the giant tree.

Then she heard a horse snorting and stomping, followed by a man's deep voice. "I know, I know."

Lenny. She'd forgotten he had a horse. Always surprising her, that Lenny.

Jane stopped to listen, afraid to disturb him.

"We're both old now," Lenny said. "Old and tired."

Jane tiptoed around the tree to find the man astride the horse on the other side of the long barn, her breath hitching inside her stomach as she took in the sight.

The morning sun lay soft and silent across the open area behind the barn while the fall trees lifted their heads to the wind, letting go of their bright red-and-mauve leaves with reluctant sighs. The big palomino tossed its creamy mane and lifted its head, nostrils flaring, then turned to stare right at Jane.

Lenny looked around. "Oh, we have company, don't we, Jericho?"

Jane inhaled the breath she'd been holding, thinking that Lenny Paxton sure did sit a horse well. He appeared rugged and windblown, his hair golden with shots of gray in the sunlight. She gave him a timid wave. "Good morning."

He nodded a greeting then guided the horse toward her, a bewildered frown on his face. "I wondered when you'd show up."

The way he said that, as if he wasn't used to people actually showing up, surprised Jane yet again. "Why wouldn't I?"

He held his hands slack on the saddle then glanced toward the fall-tinged mountains. "Oh, I thought maybe we'd finally done you in last night."

"I did myself in," she replied, rubbing her arms against the early morning chill. "I knew better than to take such strong medicine, with or without the alcohol. I don't drink."

"I'm sorry, Jane."

She remembered hearing that during the night, in her dreams, and she had to wonder if he was apologizing for what had passed or for what was about to come. "Don't worry. I'm stronger than I look."

"I can believe that." He reached out a hand. "Want to ride along?"

Jane backed up. "I've never been on a horse."

"He won't bite."

She wanted to say "But you might." Instead, she walked toward his waiting hand. "How...?"

Lenny let go of the bridle. "Just hold tight and I'll haul you over." He leaned low to cup his hands. "Put your right foot here, grab onto me and get a leg up and over."

Jane didn't know why she should trust him, but she did. And with one swift motion, he helped her up onto the horse. "Settle down against me," he ordered over his shoulder, his command laced with a husky tremor.

Jane did as he said, putting her hands around his waist. But she sat rigid in the saddle.

"Relax," Lenny told her. "Just lean on me, okay?"

"Okay." Jane thought how funny this was, her leaning on him for a change. But it did feel nice. Way too nice.

Then he clicked his boots against the horse's flanks and they shot off in the wind. The ride took Jane's breath away, making her dizzy all over again. The man made her forget how to breathe.

CHAPTER TWELVE

LENNY LIKED THE SOFTNESS of Jane. He liked the way her small hands clung to his midsection as they bounced along the rutty lane toward the backside of the big pond.

"I forgot you had a horse," she said into his ear, her breath tickling his neck and making him remember holding her close last night. "I mean, I think I remember someone mentioning horses and livestock."

She stopped rambling and grew quiet. Too quiet. He'd learned to let her talk. Her silence shouted too loud.

"He's old and ornery like me. I take him for a spin now and then, but mostly he grazes the back pasture."

"I guess this little ride will do both of you a world of good."

Lenny thought about last night. He wasn't proud of his little meltdown there in the den, but for some reason he felt lighter this morning. Maybe there was something to be said in clearing away the garbage. "Yeah. Just seemed like a good time to get away."

"Would you rather be alone?"

He chuckled into the wind, not even concerned that

sweet Jane would try to pick his brain. "I've been trying to be alone for most of my life."

"That's a non-answer," she said, her hands tightening on his stomach as the horse trotted along. And causing his stomach muscles to tighten in response.

Lenny could sense that she wanted to say more. But his Jane was well versed in restraint even if she didn't always use it. Funny, how he could read her like that only after a few days. But he knew she could read him, too, and that left him open and vulnerable.

"Jane, about last night—"

"I don't want to talk about last night." He felt her body shifting as she sat up and away from him. "Besides, it's your turn."

"My turn?"

"You know, to teach me. To show me how to enjoy life. Let's enjoy this pretty morning, okay?"

Lenny couldn't hide his grin. "Wow, I do believe we both had a major breakthrough last night."

She laughed against his shoulder, the sensation of it moving down his spine. "Yes. All it takes for me to loosen up is a strong pill and some even stronger tequila. Who knew?"

"You're cute when you're drunk."

"I just bet. But I don't get drunk that much. Like never. And Lenny, I really need to tell—"

"No, I'm serious. You're cute, drunk or sober."

"I bet you say that to all your therapists."

He sensed a hesitation in her words. Did she still doubt his motives?

"Nope, you're my first. My first therapist, first life coach, first—" He stopped, afraid he'd blurt out something he might regret. "You're first among women, Jane, that's a fact."

Her silence should have been golden, but it scared Lenny. It meant she was thinking, analyzing, pondering.

Finally, she let out a feminine grunt. "Well, you've certainly had a lot of women to compare me to, haven't you?"

Figuring this was one of her trick questions, Lenny patted her hand, holding his over it against his stomach. "Isn't that why you're trying to fix me?"

"I'm not trying to fix you. I just want to help you find some balance. That was my main purpose in coming here."

Lenny wanted to tell her she was doing the exact opposite. She'd thrown him way off balance, making him feel as if he'd received a concussion from a heavy hitter. But he fell back on his good ol' boy charm instead. "Relax, remember?"

"I am relaxed. Completely." She threw her arms up in the air, rearing back on the saddle just as Jericho shot forward. "This is fun."

One minute she was there beside him and the next she was gone. He heard her gasp, felt her feet slipping away from his, and then he felt a swish of air and heard a thump.

Jane had fallen off the horse.

SHE LAY THERE on her back, staring up at the radiant blue sky, wondering why she'd never quite mastered the art of being graceful. She could breathe, that was a good sign. But embarrassment burned through her like a singeing fuse.

She'd come out here to tell him the truth and ask him to believe her. She wasn't going to sell him out to the highest bidder, no matter how much his superagent and *Sidelined* magazine wanted her to do that. And now, she was flat on her back and afraid to face the man.

When she heard the big horse snorting nearby, she closed her eyes and prayed that she was still asleep and this dream was about to end on a good note. Mainly with her safely in bed.

But Lenny's arms tugging at her made Jane all too aware that this wasn't a bad dream.

"Jane?"

She appreciated the panic in his voice, but she didn't have the heart to play with him. "I'm okay," she said as she opened her eyes only to find him inches above her, an intense anxiety on his scarred, mapped face.

"Jane." He patted her down, which didn't help the situation. He was so good at that. "Do you hurt? Anything broken? How many fingers am I holding up?"

She squinted against his touch. "I can't tell."

"It's back to the emergency room then."

He tried to swoop her up, but she slapped his hand away. "The sun is in my eyes. I'm okay, really."

He leaned over her, staring down at her with those all-encompassing brilliant blue eyes. "Don't do that again."

"I didn't mean to fall off. I got carried away and lost my grip. And your big horse just took off."

"You like making me suffer, don't you?"

"Me? I like to make you suffer? Yeah, I plan these little mishaps just to get under your skin, Lenny."

He grabbed her then, his hands on her shoulders. "Well, you do get under my skin, no matter what you're doing. I have a real problem with that."

"I'm sorry," she said, meaning it. "I know I can be a pain." She could end this right now with the truth. He'd be hurt, but he'd survive. Or go back into that dark cave.

What should she do? What could she do? Lenny didn't give her time to decide.

"It's not that way." He lifted her up, putting his arms around her. "It's more like this."

Then he lowered his head, his mouth grazing an exploring path over her skin. "It's more like this."

His kiss was slow and steady and deliberate. His lips were warm and welcoming and challenging and punishing. At least he'd reached perfection in the kissing department.

Jane moaned low in her throat, gave up on being

coherent and professional—or honest. Eager, she wrapped her arms around him to match the way he was holding her, then she returned his kiss time and again. Over and over. Her whole body buzzed with a current that burned like the warm sun shooting down on them. Burned and hissed and shifted and moved. All from a kiss. Or maybe from a bad bump on the head.

Lenny finally let her go, staring down at her, his eyes glazed with awareness. "That didn't help much."

"Sorry to disappoint you," she managed to whisper. Then she pushed at him. "Let me up."

He released her then sank back on the ground. "You didn't disappoint me at all, but you shouldn't have scared me like that."

"You mean the fall or the kiss?"

"Both. You're scaring me a lot these days, Jane."

"You mean because I'm getting through to you, or just getting to you?"

"Again, both."

She laughed out loud, causing him to frown.

"You think this is funny?"

"I do," she said, nodding too fast. Dizzy (from the kiss), she looked up at him. "I've never held a counseling session out in the middle of nowhere, sprawled on the ground with a horse snorting at my feet."

"And a man kissing you crazy, I reckon."

"You reckon right. I normally don't act this way."

"How many of your clients have you dated, anyway?"

"I don't date my clients. That's just it. And I'm not dating you, so don't go getting any ideas."

"But kissing? Is that against the rules?"

"Pretty much. It probably shouldn't happen again."

"But what if I like kissing you?"

She gave him a big smile. "I'm learning to relax the rules, thanks to you. Not very ethical but there it is. In fact, nothing about this has been ethical. That's why I—"

"What if I fire you again?"

"You could, but we're not finished with each other."

He leaned close, snagged her by the arm and hauled her up onto his lap. "No, we're not finished. Not nearly finished. You and me, Coach, are about to go into overtime." Then he kissed her again.

Jericho snorted his disgust then nudged at Lenny's shoulder.

"I think your horse disapproves," Jane said, trying to catch her breath.

"What does he know? He's a dumb horse." Lenny got up then reached down for her.

Jane took his hand, wondering where they were headed now. She tried one more time. "Lenny, we do need to talk about last night and about a lot of things."

"I know," he said, walking with her hand in hand while Jericho gave up and grazed underneath an ancient live oak.

"You cleaned the den. That's a major accomplishment."

"I couldn't sleep."

"You cleaned the den while I slept right there."

He looked embarrassed. "Yeah, I was real quiet. Didn't want you to wake up and start bossing me around. Make me do a few push-ups or something."

"I am such a taskmaster."

Then he stopped and turned to her, his hands light on her shoulders, his eyes devoid of any illusions or trickery. "You've helped me, Jane. You really have. I saw it all there last night. All of it."

"And you wanted it to end, right? You wanted things to be normal again?"

"I did, yes. I did."

She lowered her head. If she told him about the article now, he'd backslide. Would it be so wrong to keep her secret until he was completely better? "That is a good sign. But I'm sure it was hard to come to that realization."

He nodded then looked out over the glistening water. "Real hard. There's so much I need to say."

"We have all day," she said, squeezing his hand.

"This might take a lifetime."

"We can have that, too. I don't abandon my clients once they're better, Lenny."

He gave her a peck on the forehead. "I do believe that. You're a keeper, Jane, that's for sure."

Jane glowed at that compliment, telling herself not

to get too attached. He was almost there, almost well. She'd keep working on him until he was strong again. And then she'd have to leave. They'd keep in touch, of course. But that would be the extent of things. No more allergies, no more mishaps, no more kisses, no more Lenny.

The thought of that made her want to laugh and cry at the same time. Not a good sign. Not a good sign at all.

LENNY TOOK HER to an old bench underneath a towering oak tree near the pond. "Let's sit a spell."

Jane settled down beside him then stared out over the glistening water. "Ducks." She pointed toward the other side of the oblong pond. "You have ducks."

He smiled. "Yeah, Boy loves to chase 'em."

"Where is Boy anyway?"

He shrugged. "Probably at Barbara's place. It's just over that hill." He pointed behind them to where the trail weaved into a copse of trees. "She feeds him anything he wants, so he visits her on a daily basis."

"Boy has the life of luxury."

"Yeah. This is that kind of place. I love it here."

She took his hand, surprising him since he knew she liked her space. "I was wrong about that, Lenny. When I first came here, I thought you were hiding out. But now I can see that you do love this place and it brings you a sense of peace. But you were still hiding."

He nodded. "In spite of the bad memories. Because of the bad memories."

She waited, her hand in his.

"I guess I do need to talk about all of that."

Still, she didn't speak.

"You're not making this easy, Coach."

"I don't want to push you."

"I think I need pushing."

She glanced over at him through the fringe of her long bangs. "I'm here then."

He looked out at the water. The ducks quacked and cackled as they skimmed over the pond, graceful in their symmetry. "Bertie got sick about five years ago. It started with her memory—just little things she'd forget. When it seemed to get worse, Henry called me. He was worried. She'd missed church because she got her days confused. At first, we thought it was just old age, but then the doctors figured out it was Alzheimer's. Once we knew that, we went to work on how to make her life tolerable. But Bertie didn't like being watched over all the time, didn't like alarms going off if she stepped outside. I fired more nurses than I can count. Friends kept watch—Henry, Barbara, several members of the church." He held tight to her hand, staring down at their joined fingers. "Henry came by every morning to sit with her and read her poetry. That's why he still comes by, really. He can't seem to let go, either."

"I figured as much," Jane said, nodding. "He told me he loved her."

Lenny's heart hurt with the knowledge of that love. "They could have been good for each other. But Bertie was too far gone for that. Some days, she'd go into a fit, accusing Henry of trying to attack her. It got real bad."

"Why didn't you find her a good home?"

"She had a good home, right here." He couldn't do that to his grandmother. "I couldn't send her to some strange place and I had enough money to hire the best help. I'd come home when I could."

"But you had responsibilities, of course."

"Yep. It was rough. And then came the big game last year. The Super Bowl. Do you know how much it means for a quarterback to lead his team to the Super Bowl?"

"I think I have an inkling, yes. I've seen your rings."

She'd *found* his rings, tossed on the kitchen counter. Now they were safe behind a curio cabinet's glass. Jane did more than straighten things; she put things into a whole new perspective.

"So there I was with the world watching, and my grandmother so sick she didn't even know who I was anymore. My mind wasn't in the game. I was exhausted from flying home all the time in between practice and publicity and all the hype. Then the rumors started—I was drinking, I'd mouthed off one too many times to a smart-aleck sportscaster, I'd been missing practice and I hadn't been warming up like I should. It's true I'd neglected my workouts and the coaches were concerned, but all the other stuff was just speculation. I wasn't in the best shape for a game like that, but it wasn't because of partying and drinking." He shrugged off the memories. "I tried to catch back up and make it work. I told myself if I could just win that one game, I'd quit and come home to take care of her."

"So you tried too hard and you got hurt."

"Yeah, I got hurt. But it was about more than just another injury. I let everyone down."

"You had a lot on your mind. Why didn't you explain any of it?"

He shook his head, let go of her hand to stand up and pace. "What? Tell the world that the woman who raised me was dying with this ugly disease? Have reporters and photographers camped out here day and night, hoping to get a shot of her to sell to the tabloids? I couldn't do that to her. Bertie was a very private woman. She never left the house without looking her best, but this sickness took away all of her dignity. That's why I didn't allow for much beyond the photo ops and the rumors and I could handle that as long as the cameras stayed focused on me. I played the part of a ladies' man, a shallow playboy who didn't care what the world thought, to protect my family—the only family I've ever known."

"You did what you had to do."

"Yeah, I've always done what I had to do, you know."

Jane stood to come to him. "So you lost the game

and you had to retire because you felt like the world was closing in on you."

"That and I wanted to come home to Arkansas. I wanted to be here for her. I owed her that much at least. She took me in, raised me. I owed her so much."

Jane gave him a long, questioning look but didn't ask him to explain his childhood. "I don't think anyone would begrudge you that, Lenny."

"But they did. They turned on me. Fickle, Jane. The fans and the media—so fickle, so cruel, so assuming. That day I went to the press conference for this endorsement deal and they all reported I was drunk—I wasn't drunk. I stopped drinking the day I found out Bertie was so sick. But I was tired, dog-tired. We'd had a bad night and I didn't want to leave her, but Marcus said I had to be there. For just a day. So I took a red-eye to New York and I sat down to discuss this big deal and, I don't know, something went wrong. I hadn't had a good night's sleep in weeks and I didn't feel so hot and I slurred my words and didn't make a bit of sense."

"Lenny, you were probably on the verge of a meltdown even then. Why didn't you tell anyone?"

"I couldn't. Then I would have to announce to the world that my grandmother was dying of Alzheimer's. Can't you see?"

She touched a hand to his face, her fingers like lace scraping across his beard stubble. "I can see you were caught between your life and your grandmother's last days. The world needs to know that."

"I can't… I won't do that to Bertie." And right now, he couldn't tell her the rest of the story. He wasn't ready to pour out his guts just yet. But like a stadium full of roaring anxious screaming fans, he could hear the roar of a full confession coming on strong deep inside his soul.

"Don't you think Bertie would understand?"

"I don't know. I just can't seem to stop protecting her for some reason." And he couldn't seem to go back out into that ugly world, either. Because if he ever started telling the world this story, someone would dig up the worst of it. He couldn't face that. He'd never been able to face that. And while he needed to tell Jane everything, he wasn't nearly ready enough to give her the intimate details of what had brought him to this farm when he was a child.

"So you've hidden her essence underneath a shield of clutter and disorganization."

"Yes, I guess I have. I saw that last night with you lying there on the sofa in that messy den. I saw everything through your eyes, the way you must have seen the house the day you walked in. And I felt so ashamed. Bertie did not live that way."

She put her hands on his shoulders. "And that's exactly why we have to get her house in order. To honor her, Lenny. To keep the good memories. That's all I came here to do. If we can get through this together, you can live here the rest of your days in peace and contentment, or you can go out and face the world again, knowing you did the best you could do. You just need to be healthy again."

"But that's never good enough for the world."

She wrapped her arms around his neck and looked up at him with a reassuring smile. "It can be good enough for me though. That's how you've changed me. When I came here, my goal was to get you back out into the world, to teach you to honor your obligations, and to make it known that I'd been the one to help you, but now, well, I can see that you did honor your obligations in all the ways that count. That's all I can ask. I don't care anymore about the recognition or using your name on a book jacket. I just want you well. That and a clean house, of course."

He laughed at her sensible but heartfelt declaration. "I don't know why, but you make me feel good, Coach. So good."

Then because he did feel better in spite of all the secrets still raging inside his heart, he grabbed her up and planted a big kiss on her lips. "I don't care if kissing isn't allowed. It just feels right, okay?"

"You won't get any argument from me," Jane replied right before she kissed him back.

Then they heard a dog barking. Lenny glanced around to find Boy heading toward them. With Candy hot on his trail.

"Uh-oh. Here comes trouble."

Jane twisted around. "I'll take Boy any day over Candy."

"We could make a run for it."

"With your bad knees and my penchant for mishaps? I don't think so."

"We have a horse."

"Can he outrun her?"

Lenny laughed again. "Probably not. Candy can be quick on her heels when she sets her mind to it."

"How about we stay and face her?" Jane said, giggling.

"I can do that now, thanks to you. I think I can finally tell her it's over between us. For good."

"We have made progress," Jane said, taking his hand in hers, her big eyes encompassing him with a triumph mixed with longing. "And if we stick to the plan, things can only get better. I promise."

Lenny wondered if he'd ever be able to tell her everything that had put his mind in such turmoil.

Then Jane's next words only added to that turmoil. "On second thought, why don't you take Boy and go? I think it's time I have that visit with all the other women in your life. Without you there."

CHAPTER THIRTEEN

"I DON'T THINK—"

But it was too late. Jane was already prancing with psychologist precision toward Candy. The scene reminded him of some sort of weird womanly Wild West showdown as the two stopped about ten feet from each other. He truly expected both of them to take a wide-legged stance and draw guns. It might have been hot if it wasn't so terrifying.

"Go home, Lenny," Jane called. "I'll be there in a little while."

"I just bet you will," Lenny said under his breath, a prayer for patience drifting through his mind. "C'mon, Boy. Let's get outta Dodge."

It occurred to him that he was always running away from any kind of emotional confrontation. Maybe that was why he'd allowed all of his ex-wives to hang around, and probably why he wasn't arguing with Jane about this idea. He just couldn't deal with the theatrics.

A dark memory swirled through Lenny's mind like smoke left over from a halftime fireworks display. He looked back at the two women about to square off and almost turned around, but the darkness seemed to grip him with fingers of steel. Something made him shiver. Stomping away with Boy by his side, Lenny pushed at the memory, refusing to let it surface. He needed to get back to the house. He wanted to get started clearing away the other upstairs rooms.

Lenny stopped, grabbed at Jericho's reins. "My house."

He'd never called it that before. But because he wanted to put away whatever it was inside his tired numb mind, he needed to finish what Jane and he had started. So he straddled the impatient horse and whistled for his dog.

"HE NEVER DID LIKE a fight," Candy said as she watched Lenny galloping away. "But it's odd that he didn't speak to me, even if he's mean most of the time. Even a mean man can have manners." She slanted her cat eyes toward Jane. "What have you done to him?"

Jane put her hands on her hips and ignored the way Candy towered over her like a supermodel in her expensive jeans and low-cut sweater. "I asked Lenny to give us some time alone. In fact, I'd like to call a little meeting with the entire Lenny Paxton Ex-Wives Club."

Candy tossed her hair, her smile feral. "What are you talking about?"

"I'm talking about trying to heal that man," Jane said, her voice calm in spite of her pulsing heart. "We're so close, Candace. I just need to get a little more insight into his mind." And once she had the whole picture, she'd sit him down and tell him about her little secret, the magazine articles she would never write.

"So you're gonna pick our brains, too," Candy said, following along as Jane marched up the trail. "Honey, why don't you give up and go on back to Little Rock?"

"Because I care about Lenny," Jane said, knowing that admission would only fuel Candy's fire. "He's on the verge of a breakthrough, but he's afraid to tell me everything."

"Maybe because it's none of your business."

"He's my client," Jane said, wondering why this woman couldn't see past her own insecurities. "I know you care about him, and so do Barbara and Tiffany. And even Wanda. So I thought if we all talked—"

Candy whacked at Jane's arm with her hand. "You're in love with him, too, aren't you?"

"Don't be silly," Jane said, running a hand over her hair. "My interest in Lenny's well-being is strictly professional."

"Oh, fiddle. It's okay to admit it. Isn't that always the first step—admitting that you have a problem?"

"My problem is that if I don't get through to him soon, he'd going to either push me away for good or... he'll never get back to being completely happy again. He's got so much locked up inside."

"Tell me," Candy said. "We were married close to two years and in that whole time, he never, ever talked

to me, I mean really talked to me. Ours was mostly a physical kind of thing."

"Yes, I get that," Jane said, trying very hard to block that image.

Candy stared at her. "I guess he's attracted to you because right now, you're the one enabling him. I've been through enough therapy myself to know that's what we're doing here. Now it's your turn. Just be forewarned, it won't last. Nothing ever does with Lenny."

"Duly noted," Jane said, not so sure this was a good idea after all. But she soldiered on, taking in the big square white house with the long wraparound porch. Fat ferns sat on each side of the double oak doors while pots of colorful mums and matching white rocking chairs made the whole place look inviting and cozy. This pristine house was the exact opposite of the one Lenny lived in. Glaringly opposite. "I see Barbara likes gardening."

"Barbara is the perfect domestic goddess," Candy said with a crisp snip. "And if that doesn't tell you something about Lenny, well, then you don't deserve your fancy degree. The woman is darn near perfect and even she couldn't fix the man. I'm not sure there is a woman on earth who can crack Lenny Paxton."

Jane thought Candy went deeper than she let on. Dying to ask more questions, she refrained until she could get them all in one room. A captive audience. Talking to Lenny's former wives was the only way to get the vital information she needed to put all the pieces together. Then maybe she'd be able to finally sit down with Lenny and finish her work here.

JANE FROWNED as Candy pushed a frosty frozen concoction toward her. "I can't drink that."

"Oh, come on now." Candy was already on her second one. "You can't have a good pity party about Lenny without getting a little tipsy."

"I tried that last night," Jane admitted, giving Tiffany a pointed look. "I don't drink. And besides, I'm working. I certainly can't remain objective if I'm under the influence."

Tiffany came around the long butcher block island in Barbara's huge, immaculate kitchen, her eyes flashing fire. "You're already under the influence, girl. The Lenny Paxton influence." She shrugged, swirled her own drink. "I told y'all—I saw it all the other night. The way he carried her out of the restaurant. He never carried me anywhere, including over the threshold."

Jane shook her head. "You've misinterpreted things—"

"Oh, save all the psycho-babble," Tiffany interrupted, finishing off the last of her liquid refreshment. "Look, I'm glad you dragged us here for a little afternoon gab session. We might as well get this over with." She shrugged, her baggy red sweatshirt settling nicely around her hips. "I mean, I've known for a very long time that Lenny would never take me back. We're friends, but that's about the extent of it. That and the fact that he's a silent partner in my business. Very silent."

"He's very silent on most things," Barbara added, her iced tea sweating in a pretty crystal goblet. She sat her drink down then went about the business of being a good hostess. "Here, I made these little crab cakes for lunch."

"You are such a good neighbor," Tiffany said with dripping sarcasm. She popped a crab cake in her mouth and chewed with delight.

A loud knock at the back door caused Barbara to whirl around, her broomstick skirt swishing. "Wanda, you're right on time."

"Ain't I always?" Wanda said as she strutted in wearing tight jeans, high-heeled boots and an even tighter sweater. She glanced around, her gum popping. "I take it this ain't no Tupperware party."

Barbara shook her head. "The life coach needs to talk to us...about Lenny."

Wanda's dark-lined eyes swept the room. "Oh. I'm gonna need a drink."

"I'll make it," Barbara offered, her eyes bright with a dutiful need to serve.

"I know how to mix a drink," Wanda replied. She headed across the spacious den to the open kitchen area. "I do declare, Barbara, you are way too neat to be my friend."

"I'm sorry," Barbara said. "I like things in order."

Jane lifted a finger. "Which brings me to point

222 BECAUSE OF JANE

number one. Barbara, why haven't you tried to get Lenny to clean that house?"

"He wouldn't let me," Barbara said. "Remember, I can only clean Bertie's room. I tried when Bertie was sick but he pushed me away. Told me to stop hovering. So I did. I brought food on a weekly basis and helped out when he needed me, but I gave up on cleaning the house. Especially after she died. That was a real bad time for Lenny."

Candy slinked her long body into a cushy rocking chair. "Just so you understand, Lenny never was a neat freak, but he did like things to be reasonably clean. When we were married, we lived in this beautiful penthouse in Dallas. But we had a maid."

"I kept things clean when he lived here with me," Barbara added. "We built this house when we got married. We thought we'd grow old together here."

"What happened?" Jane asked, afraid to hear the answer.

Barbara pointed to Candy. "Her."

"I happened," Candy admitted, looking down at her half-empty drink. "I broke up their marriage because, well, I was determined to get Lenny back. Only I had him back for about a month before things went south again."

Jane got up to pace around, her mineral water cold on her hands. "So he married Barbara for comfort—home and hearth, after he'd married you, Candy, but he came back to you for...a fling?"

Candy didn't even wince. "It was a very nice fling, but yes, I guess you could call it that."

Jane turned to Tiffany. "What's your story?"

"I'm the fantasy—good buddy type wife," Tiffany said with a roll of her buff shoulders and arms. "You know, the cheerleader, all-around-American girl. We met at the gym and worked out together and I made sure he ate healthy and stayed inside the zone. He did win a Super Bowl when he was married to me."

"What happened?" Jane asked, wondering when she'd gone from being professional to pathetic. But she needed to know all of it so she could help Lenny. And herself, she had to admit.

Tiffany plopped down, let out a groan then tossed her sturdy Doc Martens up onto the leather ottoman near the fireplace. "I got to be better than him at some things. I could outplay him at tennis and volleyball and since I was a track star in college I could pretty much outrun him, too. His career was waning because of his injuries while my energy level was taking off. I think my healthiness made him feel old and my competitive nature only fueled that. And then Bertie got sick. That didn't help matters."

Jane catalogued that. "So how'd you wind up back here running a restaurant that serves normal, fattening food?"

Tiffany drained her drink. "I thought I could win him back. But all that's got me is more hard work and a few meals with the man."

"Why don't you sell out?" Wanda asked with a tad too much hope. "Why don't all of you get a life, for goodness' sake?"

"That brings me to you," Jane said, turning to stare at Wanda, using her best counseling smile for emphasis.

Wanda hung onto her bar stool, her eyes going wide while she patted at her beehive. "Me? What have I done?"

Candy let out a huffy breath. "Oh, give it up, Wanda. The life coach knows you've got the hots for Lenny. And she has the bad hair to prove it."

Jane ran a hand over that bad hair but held her gaze on Wanda. "Do you believe Lenny will marry you, Wanda?"

Wanda pulled at the low sequined V-neck of her sweater. "About your hair, you don't think I did that deliberately now, do you, suga'?"

The other three women burst into laughter. "C'mon now, Wanda," Tiffany said, getting up to grab another crab-cake, "remember when I opened the restaurant and you offered to do my hair for free?"

"It took me three days to comb the teasing out," Tiffany said, shaking her head.

"Y'all are giving me a complex," Wanda huffed. "I try to do my best—"

"To ruin our hair," Candy replied with a sweet smile. "You offered me a deal once when I was between stylists and dying to impress Lenny. Remember?"

Wanda sank back onto her stool. "Okay, I guess I got a little carried away with the curling iron that day."

"You fried my hair," Candy said with a little smirk. "Antonio nearly had a heart attack when I showed up at his salon in tears."

Wanda lifted her shoulders in an eloquent shrug. "Well, I've known Lenny since grade school. *Grade school.* That's a long time for a woman to carry a torch. And I've always been little Wanda Lawhorn, the poor girl down the road he'd come to, drunk and slobbering and needing a friend. The man is a mule when it comes to his true feelings." She spiked the olive out of her martini then chewed on it for a minute. "I've always believed his lack of emotion and commitment stems from his mother abandoning him like she did."

Jane stopped pacing.

Candy sat up straight.

Tiffany lifted her feet off the ottoman.

And Barbara dropped her dish towel.

"Lenny had a mother?" Candy asked, her jeweled fingers flashing in the air.

Wanda nodded. "Of course he did. Bertie and Albert had a daughter—Lenny had to have come from somewhere, after all. But something happened to his mama when he was around three or four, and he came to live with his grandparents. The woman just disappeared off the face of the earth, or so the rumor goes." She tapped her long nails on the granite bar. "He wouldn't talk about it back then and he never, ever talks about her now."

Jane hit her hand on a table. "I knew that had to be it. He refuses to tell me anything about how he came to live here. I can't find information on the woman and I haven't been able to get Lenny to open up, but it's a classic textbook case. An abandoned little boy who harbors a strong resentment toward his absent parents. So he transfers all that angst to an almost obsessive protection of his grandparents and to the house that became his only sanctuary." She tossed up her hands. "I should have pushed him to talk to me instead of finding this out secondhand. And I shouldn't even be discussing this with any of you, but…"

She stopped, noticing the women were now looking beyond her to the open French doors. Then she heard a board creak on the planked porch.

Jane whirled and came face-to-face with Lenny.

And he wasn't smiling.

CHAPTER FOURTEEN

"BUSTED," Candy said, plopping her heels on the floor as she rose up out of her chair.

Barbara started wringing her hands. "He doesn't like it when we get together, but we've never mentioned any of this before. We didn't know this."

Jane didn't know what to say. "Lenny—"

"Save it." He turned to stalk down the steps.

"He does not like to be dissected," Tiffany said, shaking her head. "This was a bad idea, Coach."

Wanda's smile reminded Jane of a Cheshire cat. "What you got in your rule book for fixing something like this, Miss Jane Harper?"

Jane turned back to them. "Thank you for your time, ladies. I have to go."

"Yep," Candy said on a purr. "I'd say your work here is definitely done."

"No, I'm just cracking the surface," Jane said, her tone a lot more calm than her shaking insides. "I have to make him talk."

"Well, good luck with that," Tiffany told her with a wave. "He'll clam up like a snapping turtle now that he knows you tried to find out about his mother. And now that we know he had a mother—not a good thing, doc, not good at all. That subject just never came up."

Barbara hurried toward Jane. "For what it's worth, I think he needs you right now. And I think he cares about you. A lot. Somebody needs to get him to let go. None of us ever could."

Jane nodded, unable to voice all the thoughts moving through her head. Then she turned and hurried down the porch steps.

SHE FOUND HIM SITTING on the dock on the other side of the lake, his Steve Miller CD cranked to high volume with "Jet Airliner," a six-pack of beer and Boy by his side. He watched her walking toward him, his sunshades hiding his eyes. But she knew he saw her from the scowl on his face and from the heat she could feel radiating all around him.

So much for making progress. She didn't know where to begin. One of many mistakes. "Lenny—"

"You're fired. And I mean it this time. Oh, and by the way, Bryan Culver called. Your article is due. The article you're writing about me for *Sidelined* magazine."

Jane sat down beside him, her heart piercing from the pain she heard inside his anger. She'd left her cell phone on the kitchen counter. One of many mistakes. "I'm sorry, Lenny. I tried to tell you earlier—"

He opened another beer, the fizzing of the amber liquid matching the heat spreading across his face. "No, you're not sorry. You came here with a plan, remember?

You had to crack ol' Lenny. And when you couldn't quite do it by harassing me or kissing me, you had to gather all the women from my past and pick at them. I didn't even mind that, even though I told myself I should stop you."

"Lenny, please…"

"But what I hadn't reckoned on was you asking the one question you had no business asking—and not telling me this whole time that once you found out all my secrets you planned to share them with the world. You knew how I felt about that subject, Jane. And you know how I feel about my privacy. But you pried into my past anyway, in spite of assuring me all of this was confidential. In spite of me trusting you. And you call yourself a pro?"

Jane gazed down at the water. The wood ducks quacked along the shore. She wondered if Lenny's women were standing at the big windows in Barbara's house passing around a pair of binoculars.

"I made a big mistake by even considering that offer from *Sidelined* magazine," she said, wiggling her feet to steady her heart. "But I never planned to reveal anything except how I helped you reorganize the house—and that only after I told you about the offer and got your permission."

"Which somehow slipped your mind," he countered.

"I've tried to tell you. I wanted to tell you this morning. I turned Bryan Culver down, Lenny. I haven't written anything for him. He just won't stop calling me."

"And that's supposed to make me feel all better? It
doesn't."

"I don't expect it to. I shouldn't have gone to Barbara's, but I wanted to understand. None of your ex-wives
brought up your parents. Only Wanda knew and she
wasn't even sure. I just needed—"

"You just needed to put all the pieces of this puzzle
together," he said, whipping off his shades. His eyes
were bloodshot and luminous with fury. "So have you
finally got me all figured out? Ready to spill my sordid
story to the world, Jane?"

"No," she said, giving him a direct look. "No, I haven't
figured anything out. But I want to figure you out. Not
for the world, Lenny. But for me. For myself."

"You're sure dying to know, aren't you?"

Jane swallowed, took a deep breath. "I've gone about
this all wrong, but yes. I want to make things better for
you."

"Then leave. Now."

He put his shades back on, a sure sign that he was
done discussing this.

But Jane wasn't near done. "Look, you can hate me,
you can be angry at me and the world in general. I don't
care. But I do care about you. And we were so close,
Lenny. So close to truly making life better for you."

"Things were never that bad for me," he said on a
growl as he tossed the empty beer bottle across the

deck. He shook his head while the bottle rolled back and forth. "All I wanted was to be left alone. But you had to come here all high and mighty, forcing me to look back on things I've tried to forget. How can that heal a person?"

Knowing she should stop, Jane pushed on. "That's just it. You have to look back in order to move forward. You think you're okay, but you're not. I think things were bad when you were little. When you came to live with Bertie and Albert—"

He held a hand to his forehead then turned to grab her by the shoulders. "I said stop. Remember the day you came down here and found me fishing and I told you to stop? I'm telling you that again. And this time, I'm not playing games. This is my life we're talking about. And it's my business whether I want to share that with you or anyone else, understand?"

Jane wanted to pull away, but instead, she lifted her hand to his. "I understand this is painful, but have you ever talked to anyone about your parents? You've always been such a high-profile person, except for that part of your life. The world knows you were raised by your grandparents, but that's it."

"The world doesn't need to know anything else," he replied, pulling away to get up. "And neither do you."

Jane saw him stagger. She stood to help him. "Lenny, please." He'd obviously drunk the whole six-pack.

He leaned against her, a sad lopsided smile on his face. "You smell so good. You are so very sweet when you look at me like that. So sweet." His lips grazed her forehead and moved to her neck. "So sweet. But you're just like the rest, aren't you, Jane? Everybody wants a piece of Lenny Paxton." He lifted her chin with his big hand. "Here you go, then."

Jane's breath left her body in slow degrees with each feathery kiss. She closed her eyes, holding back hot tears, her mind whirling with a longing that wanted to overpower her common sense. Wrapping her arms around his neck, she drew him close.

Then Lenny ended the kisses, put his sunglasses back on and pushed away, still staggering. "Leave now, Jane. Before I make things even worse between us. I can't have you around me anymore."

Jane's heart sank. The wind turned cold as it danced across the tall pines and towering oaks. She tried to see into his eyes, but all she could see was her own shocked expression in the reflection of his shimmering sunglasses. So she turned and walked away.

LENNY CAME BACK to the house at dusk. The quiet assaulted him like the crush of a powerful opponent, hitting him with triple force. Henry wasn't reading poetry at the breakfast table. Wanda wasn't smacking gum and talking trash. Candy wasn't cooing in his ear, promising him all kinds of comfort. There was nothing in the refrigerator from Barbara, no message on the phone from Tiffany to come by and have dinner.

And Jane was gone.

He knew it even though the scent of her perfume still lingered in the air. He heard Boy whimpering out on the porch and knew that even his dog was ready to abandon him.

"There's no one left." Lenny stood in the middle of the clean, fresh kitchen, his hands shaking, his mind numbed enough by alcohol to keep the sharp edge off his thoughts, and realized his worst fear had finally happened.

"I'm all alone."

He took a deep breath, pushed at the discontent that surrounded him with a screaming clarity then walked throughout the house, noticing things he'd never noticed before. All of Bertie's dolls were now carefully displayed in a glass-encased curio cabinet at the end of the long hallway. The many books she'd loved were displayed in the bookshelves in the den and in the bookcase out in the hallway. He saw romance novels beside history tomes and autobiographies. He saw a Bible in every room, in every kind of translation. His football trophies and his Super Bowl rings were behind glass in the living room.

He went upstairs and stood at the door of Bertie's room and smelled the heady tropical lotion that Jane used after a shower. He pushed at the door then stood looking over the tidy room, watching how the last of the sun's shining rays shot out across the sunflower comforter on the bed. He'd allowed Jane to stay in this room. Why?

Jane would say he had subconsciously put her here to show her this house had once been charming and neat, instead of forlorn and in disarray. And maybe he'd purposely placed her here, because maybe, just maybe, he had welcomed her salvation.

"But you finally did her in," he said, wondering why this victory felt so bittersweet. No, she did herself in by betraying his trust. Jane, of all people, scheming to sell his soul. And hers.

Then he looked at the nightstand, his heart beating like a bass drum. Jane had left him a note.

SHE CRIED ALL THE WAY to Little Rock. It didn't help that Johnny Cash's "Ring of Fire" was playing on the radio.

I have so messed this up, Jane kept telling herself. *I should give up this life coach stuff and go live in a village in Costa Rica. I should go flip pancakes at the Waffle House. I'd probably be more help there than I am trying to tell other people how to live their lives. I'm a big joke, a hoax, a sham.*

"I'm in love with Lenny."

Jane sniffed then turned up the radio. Steve Miller's "Heal Your Heart" blared at her. "Perfect timing," Jane said on a sob. And about thirty years too late.

LENNY SAT ON THE BED, his hand trembling as he lifted the white envelope off the nightstand, his first inclination to rip it to shreds. Instead he sat there, staring at Jane's prim lettering, his mind going over her time here.

He wasn't exactly sure when he'd fallen for her. Maybe that first day when he'd watched her hobbling up the driveway with such a determined look on her face. Or maybe the day she'd fallen into the lake and come out looking like a drowned little mouse, still feisty and still willing to fight for him even when she claimed to be done with him. Jane *had* fought for him, even when he'd fought against her authority, her advice, her challenges. A real fighter, his little life coach.

No one else had ever done that. No one except his grandmother. He looked around this room Bertie had loved, remembering happier days when she would hum to herself as she went about her work. He thought of how she'd sit by the fire in the parlor and go over the lesson she'd prepared for next week's Sunday school class. Bertie had loved teaching, no matter the day of the week. And she'd taught him a lot about life.

"So how come I'm sitting here alone?"

Lenny stared at the envelope, wishing Jane had never come into his life. Wishing that she was right here beside him now. Then he went downstairs, the envelope still intact. Turning on the kitchen light, he sat at the old table, the quiet surrounding him like a soft chenille blanket. Boy whimpered, but Lenny ignored him.

Then he opened the envelope.

Lenny, I'm sorry. I've failed you. That's a strange feeling for me. Failure was never an option around my house. I had to prove myself over and over with my parents, with myself. I took this assignment as a means to impress my hypercritical parents, as a way to get my name on yet another byline for a national magazine. But I truly wanted you to trust me before I wrote a word of that story. I never signed a contract, never sent in any drafts. And in the end, I didn't care about those things anymore. It was on speculation—and after thinking it over, after meeting you and seeing your pain, I knew I couldn't break the trust we'd built. I turned down the offer. You and your health became more important than any magazine article ever could.

I wanted you to see that. I wanted you to see that I care about you. I know you're carrying some sort of dark pain and I hoped to help you deal with that, no matter what you decided to do with your life. Some life coach I am. Until I met you and all the people who love you, I didn't actually know anything much about real life. Now I do. I know about big ugly dogs, pee-wee football, horses, hotheads, dolls and camellias, and even ex-wives and old hogs. And I thank you for that. Just be happy, Lenny. I want you to be happy. And if you ever need me, well, you know where to find me.
Jane

Lenny stared at the inky words, his vision blurring, his head buzzing. And it wasn't from the leftover effects of the alcohol.

"I want to be happy, too," he whispered. And he realized there was only one way for him to be truly happy. He had to go after Jane and bring her back. But he also knew he'd have to tell her the whole story before he could make her come back.

JANE HEARD SOMEONE pounding on the door. Sitting straight up in bed, she rubbed her eyes. It was five in the morning! And she'd finally fallen into a fitful sleep.

Her heart booming with each knock, she threw on a blue cashmere robe and headed downstairs. Maybe the building was on fire.

But the fire wasn't in the building. It was in Lenny's eyes as he stood in front of the peep hole, the look of impatience on his face exaggerated through the tiny glass.

Jane whirled against the door. "Lenny's here."

Not sure what that meant—either he was going to finish her off or finally come to his senses—she hesitated.

"Jane, it's me. Open this door right now or I'll break it down. Marcus told me face-to-face you called him and quit—and he's got the black eye to prove it."

Jane threw open the door. "So you're resorting to beating up your agent now?"

She didn't get to finish her tirade. Lenny's mouth hit hers hard as she tried to take in a breath. His lips crushed hers, half mad and half glad, or so it seemed to Jane. He pushed her inside then booted the door shut.

Just when Jane had settled nicely into the kiss, he lifted his mouth away from hers. "I'm still mad at you."

"But you're here."

"I drove all night," he said, still holding her. "Drove right past that city limit sign and kept driving. I didn't like the house without you in it."

Jane blinked back sleep and tears. "I can't do this, Lenny. I mean, you can't do this. You can't just swoop in and think this is all better simply because you kissed me. I messed things up. I wasn't honest with you. I broke all the rules."

"So did I, Coach. I was never honest with you. But look, you didn't sell me out. I'm still mad about that, but you didn't do it. That helps things. And so does this."

He kissed her again. But Jane thought he was trying to kiss away the pain.

She tugged out of his embrace. "It's not enough. Not for me."

"It sure made it all better to me."

She stepped back, aching with reluctance and resolve. "We're not doing this. You fired me."

"I did, but you quit on me. So that means I can kiss you."

"No, that means you're still in denial."

"There is no denying you, Jane."

He sank back against the door then pushed at his hair. He had a day's worth of beard shadow on his face and his eyes were bloodshot, probably more from lack of sleep now than too many beers yesterday. She inhaled the leathery scent of his dark jacket and the mannish scent of him.

"What do you want from me?" she asked, too tired and drained to fight him.

"I want you," he whispered, dropping his hands at his side. "I just want you."

Jane's heart beat faster, hearing those tender words. But she knew she couldn't allow her head to follow her heart. "That won't work, Lenny."

He snagged her by the wrist. "And why not?"

"Don't you see? You're transferring all your pain into something else, just like you tried to do with all the other women in your life. You're substituting being with me for being in pain. And I caused part of that pain."

"You *are* a pain," he said on a huffy voice. "But I like you anyway."

"You like me now, yes. But soon, I won't be enough. You're trying to fill that hole in your heart and right now, as one of your exes pointed out—I'm the flavor of the month."

"I like your particular flavor," he shot back. "Your flavor satisfies all my needs."

She wanted to believe that, but she could see the defeat in the way his shoulders slumped. He couldn't love anyone until he fixed that hole in his heart.

"I can't do this," she said, pulling away. "You mean too much to me."

"I want to mean everything to you," he said.

"And I think I'd like to mean something to you. Something more than a means for forgetting. But that's not possible until you open up to me—just me. I need to know everything, Lenny. And not as a life coach or therapist. But as a woman."

He stood up straight. "Is that your best offer?"

She brushed at her hair. "That's the deal. We talk, really talk. And it doesn't leave this room. Take it or leave it."

He dragged out a long, tired sigh. "I guess I'm taking it." Then he pulled her back into his arms, his hand touching on her face. "Better make a pot of coffee. Cause I got a lot to say."

JANE BROUGHT the coffeepot into the den, along with some muffins she'd popped into the microwave. The sun was rising out over the distant hills, a shimmering pink and burnished orange. A new day.

Lenny took the coffee she handed him, holding the cup in his hand, gripping the warmth. "I never knew my daddy," he finally said. He held his head down, trying to divert the shame she could see in his eyes. "I remember the day I came to live with Bertie and Albert. I remember a little apartment in Fayetteville. I was cold and hungry, and alone."

Jane sipped her coffee. "Where was your mother?"

He shook his head. "That was always the question. Where was my mother? That day, Bertie called to check on us and I guess I picked up the phone and babbled something to her. My mother had left me alone there. She was a drug addict."

Jane put a hand to her mouth. "But you were only a child, Lenny."

He sat there, his face contorting with pain and anguish, his throat muscles working. "Yeah. I got a raw deal, Coach. But I had one saving grace. My grandmother. She drove up to Fayetteville to that filthy house and scooped me up without a word. She wrapped me in a blanket and she brought me home with her." He cupped his hands around the coffee mug. "Then I wasn't cold or hungry ever again. And I never saw my mother again."

Jane's heart had never hurt so much for another human being. "I'm so sorry." She touched a hand to his. "Have you *tried* to find her, talk to her?"

"I can't talk to her," he said, pushing up off the couch to pace. "She died of an overdose about six months after Bertie came and got me." He put his coffee down then sank back onto the floral couch. "Bertie and Albert buried her in the family plot near the house. It was a private ceremony—just us. Then Bertie turned to me and told me that she loved me and I was safe now. Later, when I could understand more, she told me she'd tried to do everything in her power to save my mother, but it was too late. I would live with her and my grandfather from now on. And that was the end of that. We never discussed my mother much after that. Bertie refused to talk about her."

Jane took a long breath. No wonder Lenny had abandonment issues, and so much guilt, too. "So you tried from that day on to be the grandson Bertie expected you to be and you've never had a chance to grieve for your mother. You can do that now. It's okay."

He dashed at the tears brimming in his eyes. "It's not okay. It'll never be right, you understand? I always wanted to talk about her, but that subject was off limits. So I've kept it that way all these years. All those dolls—they're hers, Jane. She loved dolls. I found that out when Bertie was at her worst."

Jane understood so much more now. Lenny had tried to make his grandparents proud and he'd tried to honor their stoic code of silence regarding his mother. And they'd all suffered for it. They'd brushed it away underneath the cover of a perfect façade. And he'd covered the whole thing with clutter, so much clutter.

"She was Bertie and Albert's only daughter?"

"Yep." He sniffed, coughed back the emotions. "And even though I was little, I'll never forget the look in Bertie's eyes that day at the funeral. She looked defeated and worn down. I just wish she'd talked to me more about my mother. I needed to remember, but somehow, we both managed to forget." He took a drink, his hands shaking. "When Bertie got sick, she'd call out to my mother, begging her to come home. It was horrible, but I'd ask her things and she would talk. At long last, in her delirium she told me everything. But I started resenting Bertie."

Jane reached out for his hand. "That must have been so hard, burying her child, knowing she hadn't been able to save her. And then having to relive old memories."

"I'm sure it was. I felt the same way the day I buried Bertie right there next to my mother and my grand-father." He shrugged. "I went back to the house and realized I'd never have another chance with my mother, or my stiff-backed grandmother. Bertie held her pride close, but she held a lot of pain behind that pride. She'd hidden away any remnants of my mother's existence, no pictures, no diaries, nothing except those infernal smiling dolls and a few old record albums. Maybe that's why I let the house go. I was afraid I would find something I couldn't handle."

"But you put on a big front for the world."

"Yeah, just like I'd been taught to do. I went through the motions and then that day at the press conference for the pharmaceutical company, I realized I'd be a spokes-person for some of the very drugs Bertie had taken. And some of those drugs made things worse instead of better. I thought about how my mother had died from too many drugs, both legal and illegal, and it was like I was sitting in that cold, dirty house all over again. So I bolted. It all looked tawdry and dirty in my eyes. As if I would be profiting from my grandmother's death, and my mother's death, in some sort of weird way."

Jane moved her hand up to his shoulder. "Oh, Lenny, you were having a flashback, a buried memory that came to the surface because of all the stress. No wonder you wanted to get out of that crowded room."

"I felt physically sick that day. But I couldn't explain any of it. I was too ashamed."

"So you went home and you tried to cover all of it with a messy house," Jane said, nodding. "And you held on for dear life to the people and things you could control."

He nodded, his eyes meeting hers, his face moist with tears. "I'd still be doing that if you hadn't come along."

She took his hand then tightened her fingers against his. "Lenny, I'm not going to judge you. And I promise, I'm not going to sell this story to any magazine."

He gripped her hand like a lifeline. "You're the only one who didn't judge." Then he looked at her, a solid fear in his eyes. "I need someone I can trust when we go through the rest of Bertie's things. In case I find anything about my mother."

"I'll be right there with you—just you and me." She took him in her arms and let him cry. And she cried right along with him.

THEY WERE STILL HOLDING each other an hour later. But Lenny's grief was spent now. He'd finally been able to talk about the memories that had driven him for a lifetime. Driven him and caused him to run away each time someone tried to get too close.

"What do you want to do now?" she asked, her voice hoarse and husky.

"I want to stay retired and I want to coach peewee football and I guess I'd like to keep things simple."

"Simple can be good."

"I intend to get my house in order, though."

Jane touched a hand to his chest, where his heart beat. "But first, things have to be right inside here."

Putting his hand over hers, he said on a low whisper, "I can see that now, thanks to you."

Jane was relieved to hear him sounding healthy and much more assured. "We still have a lot of work ahead."

He nodded, tugged her close. "I'm willing to go the distance with you, Coach. I want to make you proud."

"You do make me proud," she said as she laid her head against his shoulder. "We'll get through this, Lenny. I promise. But you have to promise me that you'll find another therapist and finish what we've started."

"But I like you as my life coach."

"That's not good, professionally," she said. "I want more."

He tugged her chin up, surprise coloring his eyes. "Is that our new deal?"

"That's a guarantee," she said, smiling up at him.

"And once we're free and clear—"

"Once we're free and clear and you're completely well, then I think I'll tell you how much I love you."

He looked surprised, then gave her that old Lenny

Paxton killer smile. "I love you, too," he said. "I want a lifetime contract with you, okay? No negotiating on that."

Jane pulled his head down so she could kiss him.

"Everything is negotiable, Lenny."

"Negotiate this," he said as he pushed her back against the couch and returned her kiss.

EPILOGUE

One year later

JANE WAVED to Henry and Wanda, then turned to watch her husband call a time-out before sending the field goal kicker out to salvage the game for the Warthogs. It was a perfect fall day in Arkansas. A perfect day for football.

Tiffany was calling the game up in the press box. "Folks, Coach Lenny Paxton seems to know what he's doing in the last minutes of this very important game. Remember, proceeds from this event go toward research for Alzheimer's, in memory of Lenny's grandmother Bertie Paxton. And speaking of Coach Paxton, we're lucky to have his expertise—if you want commentary on all the local sports, just tune into W-H-O-G on your FM radio dial for Lenny's lively discussion regarding everything from our Warthogs to the Razorbacks. And after Lenny's sports talk, you can also tune in to our own Jane Harper Paxton's "Ask the Life Coach" self-help radio show. Those two sure make a formidable team, don't they?"

Jane smiled as Lenny patted the fourth grader's

helmet then sent the kid back out. He was intent on the game, but he managed to turn and give her a grin and a wink. Then she felt a jolt from behind.

"So far, so good," Candy said, twirling her long hair. "I do believe he's got it bad." Then she stared down at the new engagement ring on her hand. "But then, so do I. Marcus is such a dream and he really is a good agent—got me some great modeling gigs and a couple of commercials, too. Thanks for helping me get my life figured out, Jane."

Jane smiled. "You're welcome."

"Well, I still say Lenny's in way over his head," Wanda said, her gum popping. "But I guess I can live with it. And besides, that assistant coach is easy on the eye."

"I think it's all so sweet and romantic," Barbara replied. "I'm glad he's happy." She patted Jane on the arm. "And the house looks so pretty, Jane."

Jane took all the teasing in stride. Her parents and siblings were coming for Thanksgiving. They all loved Lenny, of course. The ex-wives and Wanda all seemed to be moving on at last. Jane was settled in as the resident life coach, teaching at the nearby university and enjoying her radio show. And Lenny was certainly nicely settled into his new role as sports commentator and peewee football coach. And as her husband—a husband who was even willing to come on her show and talk about his own angst and how he'd overcome it. They were both doing very nicely in that department.

Henry pulled at his Warthogs cap. "It's a good day for football, ain't it, Coach?"

"The best," Jane replied. "I love football."

And she loved the man enjoying life out on the field.

* * * * *

COMING NEXT MONTH

Available February 8, 2011

#1686 THE LAST GOODBYE
Going Back
Sarah Mayberry

#1687 IN HIS GOOD HANDS
Summerside Stories
Joan Kilby

#1688 HIS WIFE FOR ONE NIGHT
Marriage of Inconvenience
Molly O'Keefe

#1689 TAKEN TO THE EDGE
Project Justice
Kara Lennox

#1690 MADDIE INHERITS A COWBOY
Home on the Ranch
Jeannie Watt

#1691 PROMISE TO A BOY
Suddenly a Parent
Mary Brady

REQUEST YOUR FREE BOOKS!

2 FREE NOVELS PLUS 2 FREE GIFTS!

HARLEQUIN®

Super Romance®

Exciting, emotional, unexpected!

YES! Please send me 2 FREE Harlequin® Superromance® novels and my 2 FREE gifts (gifts are worth about $10). After receiving them, if I don't wish to receive any more books, I can return the shipping statement marked "cancel." If I don't cancel, I will receive 6 brand-new novels every month and be billed just $4.69 per book in the U.S. or $5.24 per book in Canada. That's a saving of at least 15% off the cover price! It's quite a bargain! Shipping and handling is just 50¢ per book.* I understand that accepting the 2 free books and gifts places me under no obligation to buy anything. I can always return a shipment and cancel at any time. Even if I never buy another book from Harlequin, the two free books and gifts are mine to keep forever.

135/336 HDN E5P4

Name	(PLEASE PRINT)

Address	Apt. #

City	State/Prov.	Zip/Postal Code

Signature (if under 18, a parent or guardian must sign)

Mail to the **Harlequin Reader Service:**
IN U.S.A.: P.O. Box 1867, Buffalo, NY 14240-1867
IN CANADA: P.O. Box 609, Fort Erie, Ontario L2A 5X3

Not valid for current subscribers to Harlequin Superromance books.

**Are you a current subscriber to Harlequin Superromance books and want to receive the larger-print edition?
Call 1-800-873-8635 today!**

* Terms and prices subject to change without notice. Prices do not include applicable taxes. N.Y. residents add applicable sales tax. Canadian residents will be charged applicable provincial taxes and GST. Offer not valid in Quebec. This offer is limited to one order per household. All orders subject to approval. Credit or debit balances in a customer's account(s) may be offset by any other outstanding balance owed by or to the customer. Please allow 4 to 6 weeks for delivery. Offer available while quantities last.

Your Privacy: Harlequin Books is committed to protecting your privacy. Our Privacy Policy is available online at www.eHarlequin.com or upon request from the Reader Service. From time to time we make our lists of customers available to reputable third parties who may have a product or service of interest to you. If you would prefer we not share your name and address, please check here. ☐

Help us get it right—We strive for accurate, respectful and relevant communications. To clarify or modify your communication preferences, visit us at www.ReaderService.com/consumerschoice.

HSR10R

HARLEQUIN®

A Romance

FOR EVERY MOOD™

Spotlight on

Classic

Quintessential, modern love stories
that are romance at its finest.

See the next page
to enjoy a sneak peek from
the Harlequin® Romance series.

*Harlequin Romance author Donna Alward is loved
for her gorgeous rancher heroes.*

*Meet Wyatt as he's confronted by both a precious
little pink bundle left on his doorstep and his neighbor Elli
who's going to show him the ropes....*

Introducing
PROUD RANCHER, PRECIOUS BUNDLE

THE SQUAWKING QUIETED as Elli picked the baby up, and
Wyatt turned around, trying hard to ignore the feelings of
inadequacy as Darcy immediately stopped fussing.

"Maybe she's uncomfortable. What do you think, sweetheart?" Elli turned her conversation to the baby.

"What do you think is wrong?" Wyatt asked, putting the
coffee pot back on the burner.

A strange look passed over Elli's face, one that looked
like guilt and panic. But it was gone quickly. "I couldn't
say," she replied.

"But you were so good with her this afternoon." Wyatt
put his hands on his hips.

"Lucky, that's all. I just...remembered a few things."
The same strange look flitted over her features once more.

Wyatt took the coffee to the table. "You fooled me. You
looked like you knew exactly what you were doing." So
much so that Wyatt had felt completely inept. A feeling he
despised. He was used to being the one in control.

Elli and Darcy walked the length of the kitchen and
back. After a few moments, she admitted, "I haven't really
cared for a baby before. The things I thought of were simply
things I'd heard about. Not from experience, Mr. Black."

Her chin jutted up, closing the subject but making him

want to ask the questions now pulsing through his mind. But then he remembered the old saying—*Don't look a gift horse in the mouth*. He'd benefit from whatever insight she had and be glad of it.

"I don't really know what babies need," he said. "I fed her, patted her back like you did, walked her to sleep, but every time I put her down…"

Wyatt almost groaned. Of course. He'd forgotten one important thing. He'd been so focused on getting the formula the right temperature that he'd forgotten to check her diaper. Not that he had any clue what to do there either.

Pulling calves and shoveling out stalls was far less intimidating than one tiny newborn.

"She's probably due for a diaper change, isn't she." He tried to sound nonchalant. This was a perfect opportunity. Elli must know how to change a diaper. He could simply watch her so he'd know better for the next time.

Instead, Elli came around the corner of the counter and placed Darcy back in his arms. "Here you go, Uncle Wyatt," she said lightly. "You get diaper duty. I'll fix the coffee. Cream and sugar?"

Oh boy, Wyatt thought, looking down into Darcy's pursed face, his smug plan blown to smithereens. He was in for it now.

Will sparks fly between Elli and Wyatt?

Find out in
PROUD RANCHER, PRECIOUS BUNDLE
Available February 2011 from Harlequin Romance

HREXP0211

Try these Healthy and Delicious Spring Rolls!

INGREDIENTS

2 packages rice-paper
spring roll wrappers
(20 wrappers)

1 cup grated carrot

¼ cup bean sprouts

1 cucumber, julienned

1 red bell pepper, without
stem and seeds, julienned

4 green onions
finely chopped—
use only the green part

DIRECTIONS

1. Soak one rice-paper wrapper
   in a large bowl of hot water
   until softened.

2. Place a pinch each of carrots,
   sprouts, cucumber, bell
   pepper and green onion on the
   wrapper toward the bottom
   third of the rice paper.

3. Fold ends in and roll tightly
   to enclose filling.

4. Repeat with remaining
   wrappers. Chill before
   serving.

Find this and many more delectable recipes
including the perfect dipping sauce in

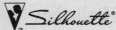

ROMANTIC SUSPENSE

Sparked by Danger, Fueled by Passion.

NEW YORK TIMES BESTSELLING AUTHOR

RACHEL LEE

No Ordinary Hero

Strange noises...a woman's mysterious disappearance and a killer on the loose who's too close for comfort.

With no where else to turn, Delia Carmody looks to her aloof neighbour to help, only to discover that Mike Windwalker is no ordinary hero.

CONARD COUNTY THE NEXT GENERATION

Available in February.
Wherever books are sold.